Playing
BY HER RULES

A SYDNEY SMOKE RUGBY NOVEL

AMY ANDREWS

Entangled Publishing, LLC
2614 South Timberline Road
Suite 109
Fort Collins, CO 80525
Visit our website at www.entangledpublishing.com.

Brazen is an imprint of Entangled Publishing, LLC. For more information on our titles, visit www.brazenbooks.com.

Edited by Liz Pelletier
Cover design by Bree Archer
Cover art from iStock

Manufactured in the United States of America

First Edition July 2016

ENTANGLED
BRAZEN

To Elizabeth Pelletier, who asked probably the world's least sports-orientated individual if I wanted to do a rugby series because she knew that appreciation of hot men in tight shorts was universal, and that it wouldn't be such a terrible way to pass my time.
That woman knows her shit.

Chapter One

If Matilda Kent had to write one more story about the latest nipple-baring bustier or test drive the newest crotchless thongs marketed to the "everyday woman" for the edification of her style column readers, she was going to strangle her boss with them.

Seriously, who paid a hundred bucks for a scrap of satin and lace that didn't cover all the bits underwear was invented to cover? A tiny string of fake pearls slung across the divide just didn't make up for the lack of fabric in a certain area. And why would someone wear them anyway? On a date maybe. But for work? Or binge watching Netflix? Or cooking a lamb roast?

Or any of those *everyday woman* things?

No way.

She clicked and unclicked her pen absently as she focused on keeping everything below the boardroom table very, *very* still in the hope those pearls would stay lax and not encroach on areas where it might result in an embarrassing urge to itch. Or possibly orgasm. In the middle of an editorial meeting.

This was not where she'd imagined four years studying English Lit at Stanford would land her.

"*Matilda.* Must you?"

She stopped clicking the pen and tuned in to the half dozen faces peering at her, including Imelda Herron, her hard-as-nails boss, who'd been in the newspaper business since God was a child.

"Sorry," she muttered, placing her pen on the table as Imelda continued.

But it was seriously difficult to listen to celebrity names being thrown around for a feature series while concentrating on her almost nonexistent underwear. Normally, she could multi-task her ass off, but the threat of imminent invasion of her lady garden by a foreign object was distracting beyond all reason.

If she was going to be violated, she'd rather it be consensual.

"Him," somebody toward the end of the table pronounced. "That's who I'd like to know more about."

Heads swivelled in the direction of the muted wall-mounted television displaying footage of a football team. The camera zeroed in on Tanner Stone—or Slick as the media called him—the captain of the Sydney Smoke rugby team.

Matilda's pulse spiked. Tanner *freaking* Stone. A close-up of him shirtless, bending and stretching, his perfect, tight ass in the air, almost made her forget there were pearls in places they had no right to be.

And the fact he was a lying, cheating scumbag who'd stomped on her heart, turned her into a romantic cynic at the tender age of eighteen, and caused her to sabotage every relationship she'd ever had with a man.

He was the reason her grandmother kept bitching at her about the lack of great-grandbabies.

Matilda would have liked to think she was mature enough

now to be over him. Sadly, she wasn't that evolved. The wound may have healed, but it wasn't all neat and perfect. It was jagged and messy and if you poked it, it still hurt from time to time.

"I wouldn't mind being rucked by him," someone muttered.

Matilda glanced around at the general murmur of agreement and tried not to remember how good the man *rucked.*

He had set a very high standard.

A surge of heat and oestrogen flooded her system at the avalanche of memories. Looking around at the lascivious gazes, she doubted she was the only one experiencing a hot flush.

"He doesn't give interviews," someone else lamented.

"He might now," Imelda nodded as the screen split in two.

One side was still *unhelpfully* focused on a pair of glutes that would have made Michelangelo weep. The other showed Bonner Hayden, a recently disgraced rugby player from another team, dashing to his car through a mob of reporters. He'd gotten drunk and disorderly and exposed himself to a waitress in front of an entire restaurant and about forty camera phones.

It had been the latest in a series of embarrassing incidents for the sport.

The attention in the room switched back to Imelda.

"Rugby's had a bit of an annus horribilis," she explained. "Their image is pretty crap at the moment. Particularly with women. They might be amenable to a feature series on one of their best and brightest—the 'man behind the myth' kind of thing."

The heat coiled and simmered in Matilda's gut now. "He's hardly squeaky clean," she objected. Best and brightest? *Screw that.* "The man's had more barely-dressed women on his arm than Hugh bloody Heffner."

Matilda didn't watch sport, and she avoided gossip magazines, but she did work on a newspaper—it was impossible to avoid stories and pictures of the one man it seemed everyone wanted a piece of.

"So? The man's a bit of a playboy. He's hot, single, and likes pretty girls." Imelda shrugged. "But there's never been a whiff of scandal surrounding him, and at the moment, that seems to be a bit of a rarity in the sport. I think the rugby board might be willing to offer up a sacrificial lamb, no matter how reluctant, to restore its image, if we pitched it just right."

Imelda tapped a finger with a long scarlet nail against her lips for a beat or two before wandering over to the large windows, every eye in the room tracking her path. The offices of the *Standard* were high in the sky with a one-eighty degree view of central Sydney. Imelda stopped as if she was admiring the sparkling harbour and the white sails of the famous opera house, but Matilda had been around long enough to know that Imelda wasn't seeing any of it. She could hear the cogs in her boss's brain working overtime.

"Sydney Smoke's Playboy Saint," she said, turning to face them abruptly, looking into the distance as if she could see the headline up in lights somewhere.

Matilda snorted before she could stop herself. "You wouldn't think that if you knew him."

A saint? Tanner Stone was the anti-Christ.

The rapt focus of the group switched instantly to Matilda, zeroing in on her as if she were roadkill and they were birds of prey. The atmosphere in the room grew predatory.

Crap.

"Oh, really?" Imelda purred, pushing away from the windows and prowling toward her with all the grace and menace of a jungle cat about to pounce. "Do tell."

Matilda swallowed. She hated being put on the spot, and

sucked at lying. Her ears were hot and no doubt an attractive shade of red, which her pixie haircut would fail to mask. "We…sort of dated."

A collective gasp rang around the room. "It was a long time ago," she hastened to add. "In high school. But I'm here to tell you that Tanner Stone is a world class jerk."

That seemed to be of little concern to her colleagues, who bombarded her with questions. "What was he like in high school?"

"Was he romantic?"

"How long were you together?"

"Oh my God," one of the marketing women whispered, "please tell me he's a good kisser. He *has* to be with that mouth."

"Oh, screw kissing," the ruck girl said dismissively. "I want to know if his legendary ball control extends to the bedroom."

Matilda blinked at the barrage of questions. There was no way in hell she was telling anybody about Tanner's ball control. She wanted this day to be over already, and it was only ten a.m. She wanted to go home, take off the ridiculous scrap of fabric and pearls masquerading as underwear, put on her favourite hipsters, and drown herself in a vat of wine.

Imelda held up her hand and everyone magically shushed. Matilda wished that would be an end to it, but she knew her boss too well. Her narrowed, speculative gaze felt like it was probing Matilda's brain with about as much finesse as a cavity search.

"Good." Imelda nodded and smiled to herself as if she'd come to a decision. "Matilda, you've been wanting to move out of fashion and onto features for some time now. Here's your chance. I want a six-part series on Tanner Stone. The man behind the myth."

Matilda gaped at her boss. For almost five years now she'd been slogging away at the newspaper. Her impressive academic qualifications hadn't meant squat once she'd gotten her foot in the door, and she'd worked hard to move up the ladder. Landing the style column two years ago had been a bit of a coup for someone of only twenty-four, but it was just a stepping-stone. Feature writer was where she wanted to be.

The jewel in the crown.

Now, it seemed, it was being handed to her—with a giant freaking string attached. Suddenly, bustiers and crotchless knickers looked pretty damn good.

"No. No. Hell no." She shook her head vehemently. She wasn't putting herself in the way of that train wreck again. "You want me to do a feature story? I've got plenty ideas. I've pitched a dozen to you over the last year alone."

Her colleagues looked at her askance. Nobody ever said no to Imelda. Matilda's pulse hammered madly at her own audacity. But everyone had a line in the sand, and Tanner was hers.

Imelda didn't do or say anything for long moments, her gaze firmly fixed on Matilda. The lifting of one elegantly arched eyebrow broke the screaming tension. "We could, of course, transfer you to obituaries. Hank is always complaining he's understaffed."

Fuckity, fuckity fuck. Matilda didn't doubt for a moment that Imelda would carry through on the not so subtle warning. She wasn't someone who made idle threats.

So she was screwed, either way.

At least if she submitted to Imelda's manipulations and delivered a stunning series, she could leapfrog right into the features team. Use it to her advantage.

If she played her cards right. But…

Tanner *freaking* Stone?

She shifted in the chair, desperately trying to think of an escape route, the damn pearls reminding her how far away she was from where she wanted to be.

"He won't agree to it," she said, prepared to grab hold of any lifeline.

"You let me worry about that."

Matilda's sigh was loud and mournful as her shoulders sagged. There was no way out of this but to quit or write about dead people for the rest of her natural life. Neither option was viable with a mortgage the size of hers.

Imelda smiled triumphantly, knowing she had Matilda right where she wanted her. "I'll set it up."

Fuckity, fuckity fuck.

• • •

"You know what this poker game needs?"

Tanner Stone looked up from dealing the last card just as Ryder Davis said, "A better dealer?" and threw his hand down in disgust.

"Chicks," Lincoln Quinn continued as he picked up his hand.

Dexter Blake laughed. "Linc," he said, "if you had any more chicks, you could start your own egg farm. You need to slow down, man, or you're going to wear that thing out."

Linc grinned. "Better worn out then neglected, Dex."

The good-natured insult rolled off Dex's shoulders. "It's called discerning, dickhead. You ought to try it some time."

Donovan Bane whistled. "Discerning. Look at you go with your big words, Dex."

"Not all football players are young, dumb, and full of come," Dex said.

"Just the ones called Linc," Ryder chimed in, and everyone, including Linc, laughed.

"What exactly do you think these chicks you're always running off at the mouth about would do if they were here, Linc?" Bodie Webb asked as he scrutinised the cards in his hand.

"I don't know." Linc shrugged. "Look good, smell good. Get our beers. Stroke our egos?"

Dex snorted. "Man, you *are* young, dumb, and full of come."

"As if your ego needs any more stroking," Ryder added. "If it took form and shape right now in front of us, it'd be a giant hard-on."

Tanner laughed. He loved poker night. Cold beer, hot pizza, and talking smack. Nothing like relaxing with his fellow team members, far away from the field and the scrutiny of coaches, team officials, the public, and the bloody media. It was usually just the single guys that made it, but it was team building at its best, and as captain, Tanner took team solidarity seriously.

The Sydney Smoke were tight, both on and off the field. It was what made them so damn formidable.

"Poker night's dudes only," he said, staring at three aces and two kings. "Now are we going to play or not?"

Tanner's mobile rang, and the whole table groaned.

"Hey," Donovan bitched. "You make us switch ours off."

Tanner grinned as he picked up the phone. "It's good to be king." The name display flashed *Griffin*. The other King in his life. "Crap," he said. "It's the coach."

He picked it up instantly. It had to be something reasonably important. Poker nights were sacred, and the coach knew it.

"Griff?" Tanner said, sliding the phone to his ear, rocking back on the chair's hind legs. "Everything okay?"

"No, everything is *not* okay," he growled. "Apparently now I'm your publicist as well."

Griffin King was not known for his tolerance. He was known for being one of the best rugby players the country had ever seen, and then for the being the best damn rugby coach in existence. He was known for being a hard taskmaster. He was known for his singular focus on his team and the game, and he hated anything that distracted or *detracted* from it.

Fripperies he called them. Griffin King hated the fripperies.

"What do you mean?"

"You're to make yourself available for a newspaper reporter who's been granted an all-access pass to training, the locker room, and the games, both here and on the road. It's a six-part series on you—the man behind the myth bullshit."

Tanner's chair *thunked* onto all fours. "The hell I am."

Looks were exchanged across the table at Tanner's vehement response. Not many people spoke back to Griff. Not even his captain.

"You think I give one single fuck about any of this crap?" Griff bitched in his ear. "You think it's my fault that some players go out on the town full of piss and wind and think their shit doesn't stink? You think I like getting phone calls from a CEO too chickenshit to do his own dirty work and tell you this himself?"

It was also well known that Griff had no tolerance for the *suits* at the top. There'd been a few over the last ten years that would have gleefully thrown him out of union. But no sports team gets rid of its most successful coach.

"So, because of Bonner Hayden and a bunch of other fuckwits who can't keep their dicks in their pants and their egos on the leash, I have to kiss up to some journo?"

Tanner knew that rugby needed the media, and he and the team did all that was contractually required of them. But he didn't believe in singling one player out from the others. One man did not make a rugby team. And he'd seen too many words twisted in the media over the years to want anything to do with a *six*-part feature.

"Yep. Suits have decided you're their man. So go do what you have to do, play nice with the journo, and don't fuck it up, for Chrissakes."

Tanner shook his head. *They couldn't be serious*. "Look Griff—"

"I'm not asking," the coach interrupted, with a voice that could have frozen a bubbling cauldron. "I'm telling you. This is one of those pain-in-the-ass, non-negotiable things you do for the love of the sport and because I *fucking asked you to*."

Tanner pulled the phone away slightly as Griff spewed fire and brimstone into his ear. He looked around at five sets of eyes, the owners of which weren't even pretending not to listen.

Fucking perfect. Just what he needed. A journo hanging around asking inane questions about shit that *did not matter* while he was trying to win rugby matches.

Six *frickin'* parts.

"Fine," he snapped, knowing he was up shit creek without a paddle. "Which paper? Who's the reporter?"

He knew most of the ones that covered the sports desks already. They were okay, by and large. Chuck Nugent was a monumental wanker who knew shit about the intricacies of the game, but he was television-based on account of his *apparently* pretty face, so at least he'd likely be spared that dipshit.

"It's the *Standard*. Someone called Matilda Kent."

Tanner was pleased he was sitting as Griff tossed that particular grenade at him.

Tilly?

No. No *frickin'* way. *His* Tilly? His high school sweetheart, the woman he'd lost his virginity to? The only woman he'd ever had a real relationship with?

The woman he'd hurt with possibly the most dickish thing he'd ever done in his life?

He knew she was at the *Standard*. He'd been following her career from afar since she landed back in Sydney straight from Stanford. But she was doing a style column—he knew that because he read it every day. How was she suddenly doing a six-part feature series? *On him?*

Tanner realised he was listening to the dial tone with no idea when Griff had hung up. He didn't like the way his lungs felt too big for his chest, or the taut bunch of his muscles in his abdomen.

Tilly.

"*Fuck.*" He threw the phone on the table, picked up his three-quarter full, long-necked beer, and drained it in a half dozen swallows.

Nobody said anything while he drank. But Linc liked the sound of his voice too much to let the silence continue once the bottle hit the table.

"You get caught on camera with your dick out, too?" he asked.

Bodie cuffed Linc across the back of the head as he said, "You okay, cap? You look kind of pale?"

Dex glanced at him. He was calm and collected as usual—off field. On field, the big guy had perfected a menacing look specifically designed to make his opponents piss their pants. "Problem?"

Oh, yeah. *Big problem.*

"Suits want me to co-operate with a journo for a six-part feature series. The man behind the myth kinda thing."

Dex whistled. "Fun. Not."

About as much fun as a root canal.

"Who's the journo?" Ryder asked.

Tanner picked at the label on his beer bottle. "Matilda Kent."

It took less than five seconds for realisation to dawn around the table. "Hey," Linc said. "Isn't she that chick you read in the paper every day? The fashion chick?"

Fuck. It had to be Linc. "She's a *style* columnist."

Linc laughed and everyone else grinned. "Sorry there, *Slick*. I'm not up on all the jargon."

Tanner had tried to convince his teammates, when they'd sprung him last year with the fashion pages, that he only did it because he liked to dress slick. They hadn't been convinced but *had* thought it was hilarious enough to start calling him *Slick*.

Unfortunately, it had stuck and been adopted by the public and media alike. Something about the alliteration of Slick and Stone had obviously appealed.

Lucky for him, people outside the team assumed it was because of how slippery he was on the field or how slick he was with the ladies. But, no, it was from following his high school sweetheart's writing career.

He sure as hell didn't want that one going public.

"That's because you're a walking fashion disaster," Tanner quipped.

"So what's the problem?" Ryder asked. "She's a chick who writes a *style* column. Make up some shit, bamboozle her with your famous charm, and send her on her way."

"The problem is..." Tanner figured it was best to come clean with the guys about his relationship with Matilda. It was bound to come out, and he'd never hear the bloody end of it. "We used to go out. In high school."

"Ah," Dex grinned. "*Now* it all makes sense."

"Oh, come on, cap. It was high school," Ryder said dismissively. "How bad can it be? I swear you're the only person I know who can dump a chick and still have them talk about how *sweet* you are all over social media."

Tanner shook his head. "Not this one. I cheated on this one." Or at least she'd thought he had, anyway.

Donovan winced. "Ouch."

Bodie also winced. "Sucks to be you."

"Dead meat." Linc grinned. "I call shotgun on your

apartment, though. This is one cool setup."

Tanner's apartment was situated on Finger Wharf, right on the harbour at Woolloomooloo. A century ago, wool was exported from the timber-pile wharf. A lot had changed.

"Shotgun his four wheel drive," Donovan said.

"Shotgun his locker," Bodie jumped in.

"Bullshit, that's mine," Dex said.

"I called shotgun first," Bodie protested.

"You can't handle his locker," Dex countered.

If he'd been in a better mood, Tanner would have laughed at them squabbling over his stuff like a pack of seagulls. But right now, all he could think about was a cute ponytail and a pair of adorable horn-rimmed glasses.

Tilly.

Why'd it have to be Tilly?

Chapter Two

Three days later, Matilda stood outside Tanner's locker room, which was accessed via a concrete tunnel in the bowels of Henley stadium, the Smoke's home ground. The fabric of the lanyard she'd been handed on her arrival scratched against the back of her neck, and she clutched at the hard plastic of her all-access pass to centre herself for a moment.

She could do this. It was her chance to score her dream job, and she wasn't going to blow it, despite wanting to turn on her heel and run. Everyone had parts of their job they hated.

It just so happened that today hers had a name: Tanner Stone.

But she was a professional, and she *would* approach this feature series like she did all her work—with dedication and decorum.

The fact she'd managed to extract a promise from Imelda that she could have significant editorial control over the series had heartened her. Her boss wanted to know the man behind the myth, and that's what she'd get.

With a side dose of how high school jerks grew up to

become adult jerks.

It would be the ultimate revenge on the guy who had ripped her heart out of her chest, and the thought of it was about the only thing keeping her from fleeing right about now.

She'd have to be careful, of course. Imelda was happy to give her leeway, but she wouldn't tolerate a biased attack. No, instead Matilda would write about how extreme popularity and sycophants had turned the boy she knew in high school into a raging egomaniac who craved the limelight and ran through beautiful women like water. There was a bigger story to be had here, as well — an exposé on society's obsession with sport and making heroes out of guys not mature enough to see beyond the adulation and excesses.

It was going to be freaking brilliant.

A burst of male laughter flowed out into the concrete corridor through the partially open door of the locker room, reminding her she was standing outside when she was supposed to be inside.

With Tanner.

She hadn't announced her arrival yet because she wanted to have the advantage. She wanted him unsettled. Because she needed to be in control here. The man had smelled better than a whole damn bakery, and she'd been like a carb junkie around Tanner Stone. Just a whiff of him had turned her into the goddamn Cookie Monster.

Going cold turkey had been hell on wheels.

So she had to remember not to get too close. To keep her distance. Although surely he didn't still smell good enough to eat. Not after two hours of training, right? She'd watched the last fifteen minutes of the session from the stands and didn't need to see it to know the perspiration would be dripping from him.

He'd be all sweaty and disgusting.

Perfect.

And she was dressed in her no-nonsense black pantsuit, which was more practical than stylish. It felt like armour, which was exactly what she needed.

Matilda gathered herself and rapped loudly on the door. "Everybody decent in there?"

The low deep murmur of men's voices cut out abruptly, and there was silence for a beat or two.

"That depends what you look like, honey." A burst of laughter was followed by, "C'mon in, baby. We won't bite."

"*Fabulous,*" she muttered under her breath, rolling her eyes.

Matilda hadn't been inside a locker room before, but she refused to be intimidated by a bunch of big, sweaty guys. Straightening her spine, she pushed the door open. A wide bank of lockers temporarily blocked the room from her view, and she stepped around them.

"I'm after Tanner Stone," she announced as her gaze took in about half a dozen guys, some still in their uniforms, some shirtless, others in their underwear, one of them, his back turned to her, was pulling on a pair of briefs, momentarily flashing her a lily-white ass.

"What you want an old man like that for?" A young cocky guy in his boxer-briefs, all meaty thighs and abs, grinned at her. Matilda was about to point out that twenty-six wasn't exactly ancient, but thighs-and-abs wasn't done yet. "They tire too easy. You need a younger model. I'd like to volunteer my services for a test drive."

Brashness in guys was usually such a turn off, but there was something so endearing about the twinkle in his eyes and the cheekiness of his grin, Matilda found it difficult *not* to smile.

Clearly he was getting laid far too easily.

"Keep it in your pants, Linc," said a mountainous-looking guy still in his uniform. He turned his head slightly. "Hey,

Slick, lady here for you."

Matilda opened her mouth to tell him she was no lady, but suddenly Tanner appeared from behind the bank of lockers, his golden-blond hair dark and wet from his shower, his chest bare, a white towel slung low on narrow hips.

"Hello, Tilly."

The locker room fell silent again as her mouth went dry as a chip. There wasn't a single drop of moisture left to even castigate him for the use of her pet name. And frankly, hearing him say it after eight years was doing strange things to her equilibrium.

Thank God she wasn't wearing those ridiculous crotchless knickers with the pearls. His voice, his chest, that towel, the thorny half-sleeve tats running from elbow to shoulder on both sides were more than enough stimulation.

"It's been a long time," he murmured, prowling toward her, drawing to a halt just out of arm's reach.

Not long enough.

Not *nearly* long enough. The incredible mix of soap, deodorant, and cologne he wore so well had her body responding like he was an original glazed Krispy Kreme.

Still warm from the oven.

Dear God…he *did* still smell good enough to eat.

He was bigger than she remembered. Bigger than he'd seemed on the telly. Taller and broader. His muscles were thicker, puckered in places, ridged in others. He looked every inch the formidable footballer with the massive kick, powerful in the way athletes often were, all leashed strength ready to uncoil.

With his slightly crooked nose, rough stubble, and brooding expression—not to mention the tats—he looked fearsome. Practically naked, there was something wholly uncivilised about him.

And so damn tactile.

She curled her fingers into her palms as the urge to touch him rode her like the devil. "Hey," she replied, finally finding her voice as she ground her shoes into the floor.

Keep your distance. He's just a job. Just a stepping-stone. *No* pun intended.

"No glasses?" he asked.

"I have contacts now."

He didn't acknowledge her reply. "You've cut your hair."

Matilda resisted the urge to self-consciously touch the back of her neck where the tips of her blonde 'do feathered so lightly. The pixie cut suited her fine hair and the gamine features of her face, giving her a maturity and authority her petite frame often didn't.

She loved it.

He leaned one huge shoulder against the nearest locker and ran his gaze over her hair. His eyes were as blue as she remembered, the dark outer rim of his iris defining and emphasising them so brilliantly. "I liked it better the other way."

Matilda's pulse fluttered as she remembered how he'd loved to see her long hair spread out on his pillow, or falling around them like a curtain when she was on top.

Damn the man to hell for putting that particular image in her head.

Resentment simmered through her veins. She needed to show him that she was in control. That she wasn't here to trade pleasantries or reminisce about the old days. For God's sake, didn't he know what he'd done had irrevocably coloured her memories of that time?

"I wonder if you know how very much I don't care about your opinion."

A couple of the guys sniggered from behind, but she ignored them. It was time to cut to the chase. She put on her best journalist voice—brisk and no-nonsense. "I take it you know about the feature series?"

"Yeah." His jaw tightened. "I heard."

He was annoyed. *Good.* If he multiplied it by a thousand, he'd be in the ballpark of what she felt. "It's a six-parter. The man behind the myth." She glanced over his shoulder at their rapt audience before returning her attention to him. "We have a lot to cover. We should figure out a time to sit down and talk."

He regarded her for a moment or two, those full, firm lips — as spectacular as she remembered — curving into a slow smile. "Oh, come on, Tilly, I'm sure you remember how *mythic* we were in the sack?"

Matilda's eyes bulged a little at his audacity, her cheeks burning as the guys behind him all grinned and high-fived. Slowly, deliberately, she slid her hand into the bag hanging off her shoulder and pulled out her trusty recording device. In the age of mobile technology, it was a little dated, but Matilda always felt like a *real* journalist with it in her hand.

She flicked and held down the record button with her thumb and brought it up close to her mouth. "If memory serves," she said, projecting her voice for *everyone* to hear, "Tanner *Stone's* dick doesn't quite live up to its namesake and pales in comparison to his ginormous ego. His fumbling attempts to manage both never quite succeeded. Let's all be glad he has more game on the field." She released her thumb. "Is that how you want the article to go down, *Slick?*"

The guys behind Tanner erupted in catcalls and backslapping.

"Whoa! Burn, baby," the guy called Linc said.

"I love her, cap," came from someone else. "I think you should marry her. Hell, I will if you won't."

"We've got a space on the cheer squad," was another suggestion.

A big Maori-looking dude shook his head. "Nah. Girl

that fierce should be the team mascot."

Much to Matilda's surprise, Tanner threw back his head and laughed, too. It was low and delicious, ruffling all the *good* places. She could see every individual whisker on his neck, and the urge to bury her face right where his pulse beat slow and thick at the base of his throat was almost overwhelming.

His laughter died as he looked at her, but there was still that easy smile lighting up his stupid, handsome face. "I knew you were in there somewhere, Tilly."

Matilda frowned. She preferred him being annoyed with her. She *needed* him to be annoyed with her. Because this Tanner—flirty, charming Tanner—was *not* what she needed.

"Don't call me that," she snapped.

He held his hands up in mock surrender. "Sorry, *Matilda*." Except he didn't look very sorry at all. "So…how do you want me?"

Matilda ignored the blatant double entendre. "I thought we could meet for six sessions over six weeks and cover a different topic, which will form the basis for that week's feature story. The first article is due to appear in next Friday's edition. Does that fit with your schedule?"

He lifted the shoulder that wasn't planted against the locker. "As long as I get to choose the locations for the interviews, sure."

"Oh." Matilda frowned, already sensing a deviation to her plans. She didn't like deviations. "I thought we'd meet at the newspaper? They have interview rooms there specifically for this purpose."

They were cold and clinical, and not full of half-naked men. There was a lot less testosterone. People wore clothes.

It was perfect.

He shook his head slowly. "Nope. That's the deal. Take it or leave it. I agree to submit"—he grinned as he drew the word out a little—"to you, on *six* occasions. But *I* say where and when."

If this was him "submitting," he'd better not ditch rugby for a BDSM lifestyle.

An image of him *submitting* whilst naked and tied to her bedpost undulated rather unhelpfully like a serpent through her brain. If only it were hissing *keep your distance* instead of *step a little closer.*

Matilda cleared her throat. She just wanted out now. She wasn't used to dealing with this much testosterone in one room. Hell, if she stayed much longer, she'd probably grow her own pair of balls.

She'd come to set up a time to meet and get the hell out. If Tanner wanted to assert himself by trying to control the extraneous details, so be it. She was the one wielding the pen.

She reached into her bag and plucked one of her cards out of the internal pocket and thrust it toward him.

"Text me with the details."

He took it and instantly raised it to his nose, inhaling deeply, and in a flash she was transported back to high school, Tanner's nose nuzzling her hair, her neck, and the sweet spot behind her ear.

Excruciatingly aware that they were just standing there staring at each other in front of a gawking audience, Matilda nodded her head, signalling her intention to depart. "Well…" She glanced over his shoulder briefly again. "See you later."

Her legs were decidedly unsteady as she walked away, the image of a half-naked Tanner, her card pressed to his nose, looking an awful lot like the guy she used to love, taunting her mercilessly.

The wolf whistles and smack talk started as soon as Matilda left the room. The guys had a great time at his expense, and Tanner let them. His brain was busy churning over his reaction to her.

Christ. He raked a hand through his hair. He'd acted like a dick again. Hell, if he'd been able to reach, he would have kicked his own ass over the "mythic in the bedroom" crack. It was hardly appropriate after such a long time apart.

But he'd been so fucking *angry.*

Angry at her for hiding behind her professional boundaries, all buttoned up with her contacts and short, serious hair and her frickin' *pantsuit,* so different from the girl of his youth with the ponytail and glasses and T-shirts with funny sayings that always made him laugh.

This girl—*Matilda*—didn't look like she knew how to laugh.

And that was on him. Kissing the cool girl at that party that night, choosing the exact moment he knew Tilly would be watching, had been an asshole move, one that she was clearly still smarting from. But it had been the only thing he could think of to make her break up with him. Make her take up her scholarship to Stanford and become the writer she'd always wanted to be instead of following his sorry ass around every regional backwater, waiting for his opening to play with the big boys.

Which could have been never.

Injury, bad luck, bad weather, bad timing—any of these could have ended his career before it had even begun. They hadn't, but now he had to live with the fact that the girl he'd once known had disappeared behind a wall that had been laid by him—or started by him, anyway.

Maybe other men in her life had been dicks, too. He cringed thinking about it. She used to shine. She'd been so happy and open, and she'd deserved so much more than having her joy sucked away by him and whatever else had conspired to make her the woman she was today.

But he had seen a flash of that clever, witty, funny girl he'd fallen in love with all those years ago.

Tanner Stone's *dick doesn't quite live up to its namesake and pales in comparison to his ginormous ego.*

Tanner smiled thinking about it. That was *his* Tilly. The girl who'd teased him mercilessly about his *hunk* rep around the school. The girl who had laughed at every opportunity.

That old Tilly was still in there, he was sure of it. She was just hiding, buried beneath a shit-ton of hurt, and he hated knowing he was, at least partially, responsible.

The thought needled like prickles on sunburn. He had to try and make amends somehow. If he'd broken her, wasn't it his responsibility to fix her? To coax her out from behind that wall so she could smile again—could be happy within herself and shine bright for the whole damn world to see?

And it wasn't about trying to wheedle his way back into her good graces, or even her bed. What was done was done and left well enough alone. Confessing the truth wasn't going to make anything better. In fact, it could make things worse. He just needed to concentrate on enticing the old Tilly out and introducing the two of them again.

Lucky he had six opportunities to do it.

"Hey, John." Tanner turned to face the guys still amusing themselves at his expense. "What's the name of that swanky restaurant at Circular Quay? The one your wife's uncle runs? With the private terrace that overlooks the harbour and the Opera House?"

About half of the Smoke were happily married. John Trimble was one of them. "Flamenco. But it's usually booked out months in advance. You want me to put a word in?"

"Nah. Thanks." It was amazing how many doors his celebrity opened. And though he wasn't one to pull strings *usually*, he wasn't above it when required.

"Whoa." Brett Gable, another married guy, let out a long,

low whistle. "That's some serious coin, boss. You wanna hope she's putting out after that."

The comment pissed Tanner off. He hated that kind of macho bullshit. His intentions were honourable, for fuck's sake. His intentions were *always* honourable. "Oh, nice, man. You kiss your wife with that mouth?"

Brett grinned, unperturbed, as Linc started singing, "Tanner and Matilda, sittin' in a tree."

Tanner kicked up an eyebrow. "Seriously, dude, how old are you?"

Linc laughed but continued. "K. I. S. S. I. N. G."

Tanner rolled his eyes. *For fuck's sake...* He turned his back on them again, which led to even more razzing. He ignored it as he strode to his locker and reached for his phone.

Next Tuesday night. Seven. Flamenco's at Darling Harbour. Text me your address. I'll pick you up.

He keyed in Tilly's mobile number and quickly sent off the message. He was adding her to his contacts when the reply came back. His pulse picked up a beat or two at the speediness of her response. He'd expected she'd get back to him *grudgingly* at some point.

I'll meet you there.

He smiled. He hadn't expected anything less. His fingers flew over the touchpad.

What kind of gentleman would I be if I didn't pick you up?

He waited for her reply, which he knew in his bones would be swift. Tilly hadn't ever been one to back down from a verbal sparring. His phone chimed, and he smiled again as he read the message.

I assume you're using gentleman in the loosest sense of the word?

Tanner tapped away some more.

You wound me.

Another speedy response.

Excellent. My work here is done.

He laughed this time, loving this glimpse of the old Tilly.

See you Tuesday. Looking forward to it.

He threw his phone onto the top shelf of his locker and was reaching for some underwear when it chimed again. Tanner smiled. Typical Tilly. Always had to have the last word.

That makes one of us.

Chapter Three

Tilly almost swallowed her tongue when the Uber pulled up in front of the restaurant. If Tanner thought she was going to be impressed by the harbour side restaurant, he was damn right. But there was no way the meagre expense account provided by the paper was going to cover this. It would all be blown in one night.

Hell, she didn't even know if she'd dressed appropriately in her little black dress. Sure, it was a classic cut that looked good wherever she went, and she knew she looked classy. Sophisticated. But she had the feeling sequins would be more appropriate.

And diamonds.

Unfortunately, the only sparklies she owned were of the cubic variety.

She glanced to her left. The elegant arc of a white sail, illuminated to show off the perfection and splendour of Sydney's famous opera house, glowed in the foreground.

So this was how the other half lived.

"Tilly!"

Matilda turned to find Tanner approaching, her annoyance at being called Tilly evaporating as his big frame, looking surprisingly civilised tonight in a black suit, snowy white shirt, and trendy tie, drew closer.

There was, however, still something of the animal about his mane of golden-blond hair and his powerful stride that no veil of respectability could mask.

"You look lovely," he said, leaning in to drop a peck on both cheeks before she could even gather herself to avoid it.

She stared at him for a moment or two, dumbfounded, when he pulled back. The Tanner she'd known hadn't been this...cultured. "How very *French* of you," she muttered.

He grinned. "I'm a man of the world now, didn't you know? Spent six months in France when I was twenty, playing over there."

Yes. She knew. She'd surreptitiously followed his career over the years, despite telling herself she wouldn't.

"Although to be honest," he continued, sliding a hand onto her elbow and guiding her toward the restaurant, "I much prefer a different kind of French kissing."

Tilly's heart rate spiked, and she stumbled slightly. Tanner seemed not to notice, although he did tighten his grip slightly while she regained her footing. They were almost at the door before she'd recovered her senses enough to protest.

"Stop, Tanner," she said, shrugging her arm out of his grasp.

He quirked an eyebrow. "Problem?"

"Yes," she said, ignoring the slight hitch in her breath caused by that eyebrow. *For the love of all that was holy, how on earth could an eyebrow be sexy?* "We can't eat here."

He frowned. "Why not? It's one of the best restaurants in the city. It has a Michelin star, and a view to die for."

"And a price tag to go with it, I bet. Newspaper expense accounts are not what they used to be, and this place will blow mine out of the water."

He chuckled then, deep and low, his nose looking less crooked as his face creased with laughter. He took her elbow again and urged her onward. "I'm taking you out to dinner, Tilly. I don't expect you to pay for it."

Matilda ground her feet into the pavement, refusing to be jollied along like some hapless female starstruck by his company. "This isn't a *date*, Tanner. It's an *interview*."

"I don't care what you want to call it, Tilly. I'm the man. We're eating together. I'm paying. Simple as that."

Matilda blinked. His sentiment shouldn't surprise her. He'd always been the kind of guy who opened doors, stood back to let her pass, and paid for her wherever they went, even back when he was surviving on his weekend-shelf-packer earnings.

But this was a whole other level. Putting her feminist affront to one side, it was important not to cede any of the power to him. She had to control how these interviews went, she couldn't let him lord it over her.

"Don't call me, Tilly."

If he saw the gathering storm flashing in the amber flecks of her blue-green eyes, he didn't pay it any heed. "If I'm picking the locations, then I *will* cover any costs incurred." He shoved his hands in his pockets. "That's a deal breaker. Take it or leave it."

"Nice try. But you and I both know this has come from the top. You're as much a pawn here as I am."

"If you think I won't tell them to go *fuck* themselves, then you're dead wrong."

Even without his menacing tone and the determined slash of his mouth, Matilda believed him. She ground her teeth. She hated that ultimately he held the upper hand. That she needed him more than he needed her. That her career path was dependent on this feature series.

She changed tack. "How about we go Dutch?"

"How about we don't."

Matilda gave an aggravated sigh, knowing she was snookered. "Fine."

She had a good mind to order the most expensive thing on the menu, but she didn't have it in her to be so bitchy. Being raised by an old leftie grandmother, and coming from a working class background, it was still somewhere in her DNA to be suspicious of wealth and excess.

"Thank you," he smiled.

It was in his favour that there wasn't anything triumphant in his tone. He reached for her elbow again, but she pulled out of reach. He might be calling some of the shots, but he didn't get it all his way.

He grinned at her, clearly unconcerned by her recalcitrance. Or, as her grandmother would have called it, petulance.

"After you," he gestured.

Matilda entered the restaurant and was greeted politely by the maître d'. It was an entirely different matter when Tanner followed her inside. Clearly, the headwaiter recognized him, and much obsequiousness and fuss ensued. Which would have been comical enough without half a dozen stops for autographs and selfies with an admiring clientele.

It obviously didn't matter how posh you were—celebrity appealed to everybody.

By the time they were seated on the terrace—conspicuously absent of other tables—half an hour had elapsed.

"Sorry about that." He grimaced, not looking very sorry at all. Looking quite pleased with himself, actually.

"That's okay," she said, feigning boredom. "I took notes while your groupies stroked your ego."

His low chuckle was both unexpected and sexy. It was

irritating that she couldn't rile him as easily as his mere presence was riling her. "I remember when you used to tease me about my groupies."

He was right. *God.* She was turning into such a freaking shrew! Whatever their personal history, he'd done well for himself, and he *should* be proud of that. Hell, somewhere deep down, if she pushed past old hurts and resentment, she could admit that she was proud of him, too.

He'd had a goal, and he'd worked hard and achieved it. Unlike her, who was still a long way from being professionally accomplished.

Although hopefully that was about to change.

Thankfully, with the arrival of the maître d' himself to take their drinks order, she didn't have to answer.

"Do you like champagne?" Tanner asked.

"Yes."

He smiled at the hovering maître d'. "I'll have your best bottle of champagne."

Matilda frowned. "You drink champagne?"

"No. I drink beer."

"I'm not going to drink a whole bottle of champagne, Tanner."

"Never say never," he grinned.

Matilda didn't know how much the best champagne in this restaurant might cost, but with the opera house looming large behind Tanner's head she figured it was way beyond anything she could afford. She looked at the waiter. "Just something cheap will be fine. I'm more of a cask wine girl. Quality is wasted on me."

The waiter's polite facade was sorely tested at her mention of wine that came in a cardboard box, but it didn't matter, as Tanner gave a dismissive shake of his head and said, "You're best please. And whatever boutique beer you recommend."

"Yes, sir," the waiter beamed and departed with a skip in

his step.

Matilda arched an eyebrow at Tanner. "Only the best for you, huh?"

"What's the point in having money if you can't spread the joy?"

Matilda regarded him steadily. Tanner was clearly enjoying the spoils of his career.

And more than a little eager to show them off…

"Rugby's made you rich, huh?"

"Rugby pays me well. My financial guy makes me rich."

It was surprising to hear Tanner admit it so openly. She'd have thought he'd be more guarded in front of a journalist. Sure, he'd always been a bit of an open book, but he must have learned over the years that the media could be his best friend or his worst enemy.

And therein lay the problem, she suspected. He just didn't see her as a journalist. He wasn't taking her seriously. And that just wouldn't do.

Time to remind him.

"Let's get down to it," she said briskly, straightening her shoulders as she reached into her small black clutch purse. She was conscious of him eyeing her, the smooth lines of his forehead furrowing a little as she pulled out her recording device.

"What's the rush, Tilly? I prefer a little foreplay before *getting down to it*. I seem to remember you used to as well."

Matilda almost dropped her recorder, shooting him a sharp glance. A retort came to her lips, but she could see the amusement dancing in his blue eyes. He was teasing her, testing her, maybe. Or maybe he was still pissed about being press-ganged into these interviews, and this was some kind of passive-aggressive bullshit.

For sure he was trying to rattle her.

Fine, two could play at that game.

"I'm more the wham, bam type now."

The slight widening of his eyes and his sudden swallow brought her a measure of satisfaction. She placed the tape recorder in the centre of the table. "Do you mind if I record…"

"Us getting down to it?" He smiled, recovering quickly. "Sex tapes are expressly forbidden, but the rugby bigwigs did say I had to accommodate you in every way possible, so…" He shrugged. "I'm willing to break some rules."

Matilda gritted her teeth. She would not rise to his bait. "The interview," she clarified.

"You know…you're not as much fun as you used to be."

That was neither fair nor true. She might be more guarded now, but she knew how to have fun. Just not with Tanner. There was too much history, too much muscle memory, to drop her guard around him.

She shrugged. "You're not as funny as you used to be."

He grabbed his chest as if she'd wounded him, but chuckled nonetheless. "Touché."

More French.

Thankfully the maître d' arrived with their drinks, providing a circuit breaker for the puzzling swirl of tension that crackled and pulsed around them. She vaguely listened to Tanner chatting with him about the Smoke's chances for the top eight as she tried to figure it out.

Why was he pretending to flirt and pushing her like this? It wasn't helpful. In fact, it was downright annoying. And what was with her heightened awareness of him as a man, which was completely contradictory to her feelings?

Objectively it made sense, of course. Tanner was a sexy, confident guy. But there was a terrible familiarity to the jitter in her belly and the skip in her pulse.

Too familiar.

Oh, crap.

It was a shitty time to realise this physical response wasn't *just* about Tanner's sexual appeal to women generally but his appeal to her *personally*.

As a woman who knew him intimately.

Fuckity fuck. How could her body betray her like this?

She didn't want it. She sure as shit didn't need it. And it was utterly pointless. She could never be with Tanner again, a guy who'd treated her so badly. No matter how much her traitorous hormones were curled up and purring in her belly.

Maybe one day she could forgive him, but she'd never forget that night. Her sense of betrayal ran too deep.

It wasn't just that he—*her boyfriend*—had been all over another girl. It was the identity of the girl.

Jessica Duffy.

Popular girl. Cool chick. Hot babe.

Queen bee of the in crowd, and she knew it. The one that all the guys had their tongues out for. Who'd flirted outrageously with Tanner at every opportunity. But she'd also been a mean girl, snobby and merciless in her disdain for those she considered beneath her.

As a somewhat bookish teenager from a poor family, Matilda had been one of many in Jessica's crosshairs. Reasonably resilient, Matilda had shrugged it off. She had friends and was generally well liked. The odd "nerd-girl" barb from Jessica was relatively easily ignored. Even her desperate attempts to snag Tanner hadn't worried Matilda. Secure in his fidelity, they'd just seemed funny.

Boy, had that been monumentally stupid.

Tanner kissing another girl had been gutting. Kissing mean-girl Jessica had heaped insult on injury.

And he didn't get to flirt his way out of that, no matter how much her body bitched at her. She was here for information. For her gutting exposé of the mythical Tanner Stone. For her future career. Everything else was ancient history.

Tanner asked the maître d' to take their meal orders while he was there. He ordered an entrée of oysters and followed it with a main of lobster. As a teenager, hungry to hit the big league, he vowed he'd enjoy whatever came his way if he did eventually break through, and oysters and lobster were a symbol of how far he'd come.

He'd grown up the eldest of four kids in a working class family in a small town about a thousand kilometres from the ocean. Lobster had never been part of his vocabulary. To be able to bring Tilly here and show her how far he'd come, share his success with her, was the ultimate.

She ordered the risotto after an inordinate amount of time spent choosing. If he didn't know better, he'd say she was trying to figure out what was the cheapest thing on a menu that didn't come with prices for a very good reason. Either way, it'd had given him longer to check her out.

The light on the balcony was subdued to emphasise the view just over his shoulder, with only a low candle burning on the table between them. But it burnished the tips of her wispy, blonde pixie cut and threw her face into flickering relief.

It was familiar and yet not. Shadows fell in the hollows beneath cheekbones more prominent than he remembered. She'd always been petite—he'd felt like a giant beside her— but cheeks that had once been fuller were now spare. Her chin was pointier, her mouth more noticeable.

A very *distracting* thought.

Almost as distracting as her dress. The shoestring straps, perfect for a sultry Sydney night, showed off her delicate collarbones and shoulders, and the shortness of her hair exposed her throat and the bareness of her nape. It wasn't one of those dresses that hugged every inch of a woman's body. It skimmed rather than clung, and left a lot to the imagination.

Tanner liked that. He had a very good imagination. And an even better memory. It sure as hell beat the pantsuit from last week.

It was her dress that had done it. He'd come here tonight determined to cooperate. To set her at ease and by doing so, draw her out, make her laugh a little. But then he'd laid eyes on her in that dress and it had taken him one second to realise he wanted her back.

Yes, he'd screwed up. Big time. Yes, he had a lot of making up to do. But he hadn't realised how much he'd missed her. Until now.

And he was determined to win her back.

So he'd started flirting with her. The results so far had been encouraging. She didn't seem so sure of herself anymore.

"Okay, let's begin, shall we?" she said as the maître d' departed, her serious journo voice back in play, and she pushed the record button on the Dictaphone.

He hated that voice already.

"You want to start at the very beginning? It's a very good place to start."

She was the only woman he'd ever met that had seen *The Sound Of Music* at least fifty times, and he wasn't above using intimate knowledge of her to try and earn his way back into her favour.

The reference had to be worth a grudging smile, right?

"No."

No? *Tough audience.* But then she wouldn't need him to start there, would she? Because she knew the beginning part. Intimately.

"Let's start after—" She faltered for a second, her gaze dropping to the starched linen tablecloth before rising again, glittering with determination. "After I went to Stanford."

They chatted all through dinner. Tanner resolved to be on his best behaviour and didn't even push a third glass of champagne on her when she refused. He wasn't keen on talking about himself, but it was a means to an end. Once the questions were out of the way, he could flirt some more. The more he stuffed around during, the longer it would take to get to the good bit.

By the time the maître d' had cleared the table of their dessert plates—and earned himself some prime tickets to a Smoke game Tanner just happened to have in his jacket pocket, for fitting them in at such short notice—he'd related his rugby journey from small regional feeder teams to his sojourn in France. Mainly, she'd let him talk, only interjecting a question every now and then for clarity or further information.

"I think that'll do for now," she said, checking her watch before leaning across to turn off the recording.

Tanner relaxed. Now the fun could begin. "Good. Now for my questions."

She quirked an eyebrow at him. "Your questions?"

"Sure. You've had an hour and a half. Don't I get a turn?"

"No."

"You like saying no, don't you?" he teased.

"To you? Yes."

Tanner laughed. "You're bad for my ego."

She shoved the Dictaphone in her clutch. "I think your ego can stand it."

"Okay, fine. How about just one? Then I'll drop it."

"That's not how this works."

"Humour me."

She shot him a deadpan look. "Don't you have a guy for that, too?"

Tanner grinned. "You know I can harp on about this for the rest of the night, right?"

Her expression told him she absolutely knew. "Fine," she huffed. "One. *Nothing* to do with us."

He sucked in a whistle. "Tough girl, huh? I like."

"You should. It's your handiwork."

There was no particular accusation in her voice, but her barb hit its mark. "Tilly…"

"Goddamn it, Tanner, it's Matilda," she snapped. "Now ask your damn question."

Tanner hated how far up her walls were and was just pissed off enough—at himself as well as her—to be reckless.

"Are you wearing some of those crotchless panties I've been reading about in your column?"

If she was outraged or disgusted at his deliberately provocative question, she hid it well. Only the slight widening of those big, blue-green, opal-like eyes betrayed her reaction.

"Why?" she asked, her voice steady. "You have some kind of women's underwear fetish you want to talk about?"

Tanner chuckled as she fished around in her purse. If he were going to wear underwear for any woman, it'd be for her. She pulled out the Dictaphone and hit record again, pointing it in his direction.

She plastered a faux delighted smile on her face. "I'm sure the guys in the locker room would *love* to know."

"Thanks," he laughed again. "I like to keep my fetishes private."

Her smile slipped as she withdrew her hand and slid the device back in her bag. The clasp shut with an audible click, and she glanced at him. "You read my column?"

Tanner nodded. "I've *always* read your column."

Her chin dipped down as pink crept across her cheekbones. The fingers of her left hand fidgeted with her discarded napkin. "It's not exactly where I thought I'd end up while I was studying at Stanford."

She was apologising? His gut squeezed at the display of vulnerability. *This* was the real Tilly. He slid his hand across the table and over the top of hers. Surprisingly, she didn't withdraw. "I like it."

She smiled then. Grudgingly. But it was her first genuine smile of the night, and his lungs suddenly felt too big for his chest.

"Get all your style tips from me, do you?"

"Absolutely." He grinned. "I love your practical, no-bullshit, irreverent style of writing. Is that how you're going to write about me?"

"Oh, no," she said, withdrawing her hand from his. "Feature writing is *serious*"—she made some air quotes—"journalism."

"So there'll be no bullshit?"

She shook her head. "Absolutely not. It will be the complete and utter ungarnished truth."

That's what Tanner was afraid of.

Chapter Four

"This is me," Matilda said as the Uber pulled up in front of her apartment building in the *un*-gentrified end of Potts Point, her pulse all aflutter from Tanner's thigh being pressed up against the length of hers for the duration. He'd insisted on escorting her, then insisted on sitting in the back, even though the car that had shown up he could probably pick up and shove in his pocket.

Thank God she hadn't had far to go.

She practically sprang out of the vehicle to get away from him. His cologne had been wrapping her up in sticky tentacles, and it had been an exercise in self-control not to turn her face into his neck and inhale how good he still smelled.

She wasn't sure what he was wearing these days, but she was pretty sure it was the French word for "melts women into puddles."

Unfortunately, Tanner followed her out of the Uber.

"What are you doing?" she demanded as the car drove off.

"I'm seeing you to your door."

"I'm fine," she dismissed.

He sighed patiently. "If you don't mind me saying," he said, looking up at the facade of her ten-story building, with the faded and peeling white paint, and the splashes of graffiti, "this isn't exactly the most salubrious area. I'd feel better knowing you got inside safe and sound. In case there are any…undesirable elements hanging around, lurking in the hallways."

"You think Bonner Hayden's going to jump out from around a corner and wiggle his wang at me?"

He laughed. "I'm pretty sure he's wiggled his last wang."

Matilda doubted it. He'd only copped a fine, not even one lousy match suspension. "Look. It's okay. Really. The neighbourhood might seem a little dodgy, but I've been here for five years, and it's mainly older residents who have been here for fifty. It's perfectly safe. Go home."

He folded his arms. "I'm going to have to ask you to humour me a little more."

He sounded like a policeman—polite but unshiftable. All he needed was the "ma'am."

She knew from experience that Tanner couldn't be physically moved—he was too damn big. And she so did not want to be having this conversation on the footpath.

"Suit yourself." She shrugged, turning on her heel and walking up the pathway to the glass entry doors, through the shadows of an overarching avenue of Jacaranda trees.

"They need to put better lighting out here," Tanner griped as he followed. "Anybody could be lying in wait."

Matilda ignored him as she headed for the entrance, grateful when she was able to push them open and step inside. There was no doorman—it wasn't that kind of place—just rows and rows of mailboxes and an ancient lift.

"Satisfied now?" she asked, turning to face him as she pushed the lift button. She could tell from the light above it was on the ground floor, but she knew from experience it took the doors a while to crank open. "Safely inside."

He shook his head. "I said I'll see you to your *door*."

Irritation prickled under her skin. She'd been coming in and out of her apartment without an escort for a long time—day and night. If he'd been flirting with her all evening in the hope of ending up in her bed, he was sorely mistaken.

"If this is some ploy to get into my apartment and then into my pants, you're completely delusional."

"I was thinking more along the lines of checking for hidden ninjas."

The lift door cracked open on a groan.

She folded her arms and tapped her foot. She wasn't in the mood for his jokes. He held his hands up in mock surrender, a slight smile playing on his lips. "I promise I won't even try to"—his gaze dropped to her mouth—"kiss you."

Matilda's mouth tingled under his intense scrutiny, and all she could think about as the lift opened, inch by noisy inch, *was* Tanner kissing her.

She'd been kissed by other men. Some had been most excellent kisses, even if none of them had worked out. But this was Tanner, her first love—the gold standard of kissing. And her body was melting down at the memories.

She escaped into the lift as soon as the gap was wide enough to allow it. "I'm not sure you'll fit in here," she said and really hoped it was true. "It's possibly the world's smallest lift."

"I'll manage." He strode in undeterred, dominating the space, sucking away all her air.

Matilda punched the floor ten more times than necessary, keeping her eyes trained to the front, hyperaware of Tanner, sprawled casually against the opposite wall, his hands-in-pockets stance exposing a splash of white shirt pulled taut across his abdomen. She crowded forward, closer to the control panel, desperately trying to keep as much distance between them as possible as his cologne swirled around her.

He smelled like orchids and…ouzo.

The door slowly ground shut, protesting all the way, and Matilda willed it to—just this once and she'd never ask again—deliver her speedily to her floor. As was its custom, the lift stood still for long moments before finally grumbling to life.

She stared straight ahead as it slowly ascended, desperately trying to think about anything other than him kissing her. And failing. How could she not, when she was excruciatingly conscious of him standing all big and solid and silent in her peripheral vision, staring at her, his gaze heavy on the patch of skin where her neck joined her shoulder as if that might be the place he'd like to start.

It was warm and getting warmer in the lift, but still her nipples beaded as if they were standing in a fridge. And for all the room in here, they might as well have been.

She hated that her body had so easily gotten over his Judas kiss. That she was a slave to her hormones. Or maybe it was her memory.

The emergency telephone panel was right in front of her, and she concentrated on that instead of his relentless gaze. She wondered if she picked it up and ordered some amnesia stat whether that would be considered misuse of public property.

"You could get up to a lot in a lift that moves this slow."

His words rumbled out into the small space, and Matilda swore she could feel each one of them glide over her skin. Her pulse fluttered madly as an image of them going for it against the wall—his trousers open, her skirt rucked up—filled her head. She spoke quickly, unthinkingly, to dispel it.

"It's faster going down."

He chuckled, causing goose bumps *everywhere*. "Clearly it has its priorities *all* wrong."

Matilda swallowed. Damn it. It seemed Tanner could turn anything into sexual innuendo. He'd never been this suggestive as a teenager. Not in front of her, anyway.

She decided ignoring him was best. As much as she could while stuck in the world's smallest *and slowest* lift.

Finally, after a silence that stretched to breaking point, the lift settled on the top floor with its usual exaggerated shudder. Of course, they had to wait for the grindingly slow mechanism of the door to open, but once it had, Matilda was out of there.

He was behind her, she could sense it, but at least now she could breathe again, her lungs expanding rapidly, dragging in much needed air.

Her apartment was almost at the end of the poorly lit hallway. Every second bulb was blown and the carpet was threadbare. She covered the distance between the lift and her front door as quickly as she could without breaking into a run. Her key was in the lock and her hand was on the knob by the time Tanner, moving at a more leisurely pace, finally ambled closer.

She was almost home free, without licking his neck or doing him against the wall of the lift. All that was left was to turn the key and push the door open. She opened her mouth to thank him and send him on his way, but there was something about the intensity of his gaze that seemed to hold her in his thrall. She could *feel* it on her nape as if he was touching her there.

Her brain was telling her mouth to say good night and her legs to move inside her apartment, but the rest of her body wanted to turn toward him, reach for him.

To hell with their past.

He halted behind her, and the fine hairs on her nape stood to attention as the weight of his gaze zeroed in on that same spot it had during those long moments in the lift.

"You look good, Till," he said, his voice rough and low,

dropping into that intimate register she recognised even after all these years.

The words went straight to her belly, melting and tightening it all at once.

She looked over her shoulder at him as if the hands of time had given her a tap. The retort, *don't call me Till*, died on her tongue as her hormones completely hijacked her senses.

She was a woman again, instead of the ex he'd done wrong.

She turned slightly, leaning a shoulder into her door and cocking her eyebrow. "Even without the ponytail?"

Matilda injected a lightness into her voice. She didn't want him to know that his crack about not liking her hair had rankled. And then it had pissed her off that it had rankled.

She shouldn't give a rat's arse what he thought of her hair.

But somewhere deep in her X chromosomes, she did.

He moved closer and her breath hitched. He rested his big shoulder against the doorframe. For any normal person the distance would have been respectable. But he was a big guy, which narrowed the gap significantly. There wasn't much between respectable and *reckless* at the moment.

He lifted a hand to her wispy fringe, brushing it with his fingertips, following the curve of her face. Goose bumps fanned down her neck and across her shoulders.

"I changed my mind," he murmured, tucking a short strand behind her ear. "I approve."

Matilda's eyes fluttered closed briefly as his fingers drifted to her cheekbone. For a light caress it was packing an almighty punch. "I don't need your approval," she whispered, the sensible urge to pull away battling with the *in*sensible urge to turn her cheek into his palm.

The pad of his thumb feathered along her jaw. "I know."

"You don't have any say over what I do with my hair," she asserted. She had to assert *something* because her body was not remotely holding the high ground.

In fact, it was dissolving beneath his touch, her breath thick in her throat, her pulse one long, slow thud after another.

"I know." His thumb brushed toward her chin. Had he moved closer? Or had she?

Matilda swallowed. "You *never* did."

"I know." His thumb traced her bottom lip, his gaze wholly intent on the process, staring at her mouth like it was more fascinating than Saturday night's game play.

Her body flamed beneath the erotic stroke. She could feel it rasping against her nipples and tingling between her legs. His other hand slid up to her face, his other thumb joining in the bottom lip torture.

Just as Matilda thought she couldn't take another second, he lowered his head toward her. Slowly. Slowly. His scent invaded every cell, muddling her senses. How could she want him to kiss her after Jessica freaking Duffy?

But, she did. God help her, she did.

His mouth was a whisper from hers when she panicked. Since when did she let her body dictate to her?

"I thought you weren't going to try and kiss me?" she murmured.

He halted, stayed very still, his hands still cradling her face, his mouth almost touching hers. There was beer on his breath and a heady sweetness in the liquorice of his aftershave.

"I'm not," he murmured, his hands sliding from her face as he pulled away, straightening his back and shoving his hands in his pocket.

Matilda was glad for the solidness of the door after his abrupt withdrawal. Her entire body sagged from the break in tension, and without it, she may well have slid to the floor. In fact, it was still a real possibility.

She sucked in some choppy breaths to shunt some oxygen to muscles badly in need of it, as lust and desire churned and mixed like a kaleidoscope in her gut.

She glanced at him to find him wearing a stupid smile on his stupid face, *obviously* very aware of the effect he'd had on her.

Obviously very pleased with himself.

This was not the way she pictured this night would end. A polite handshake maybe. But in less than three hours in his company she'd been a whisper away from pashing his face off in the corridor outside her apartment.

And God knew where it would have ended up, seeing as how she'd obviously lost her mind where Tanner was concerned.

"Sweet dreams, Matilda." He grinned as he pushed off the doorway. "I look forward to the article on Friday."

She frowned at his retreating back. The easy grace of his big frame and the cockiness of his swagger were irritating as hell when she could barely coordinate her fingers to turn the key in the lock.

Tanner Stone was way too sure of himself. Too many women had been letting him have it all his own way.

If he thought he was going to walk out of here all cat-that-got-the-cream, he was dead wrong. "The answer is no," she called out.

He stopped. Turned. Smiled. "No?"

"The crotchless undies? Not wearing them." She pushed her door open. "I'm not wearing anything at all."

Matilda was grateful, as the door clicked shut behind her, that there were only a half dozen paces to her couch. She collapsed onto it, her legs shaking.

If there *was* a hidden ninja in her apartment, she was totally screwed.

• • •

The next morning, Tanner woke to major traffic on his Twitter stream. That wasn't unusual. But it was for a Wednesday morning. One of his followers—@rugbybunny1—had tweeted a picture of him and Tilly sitting at their table last night. They appeared to be holding hands. It was slightly grainy, but even in profile it was undeniably them.

> Spied this cute couple out and about last night. Who is the mystery woman @slickstone? #sydneysmoke #holysmoke #mightbelove

His largely female following had gone crazy speculating and retweeting. It had taken them all of about an hour to track the mystery woman down.

Somebody called @slickstonesmistress had tweeted

> Looks like #style columnist @MatildaK #holysmoke #betternotbelove #handsoffmyman

Tanner grinned as he scrolled through his feed. Tilly was just going to love being dragged into that. He contemplated joining in the fun, dropping some teasing hints, but he knew too well by now not to encourage the crazy that frequented his Twitter stream.

Then he remembered Tilly's quip about her lack of underwear from last night and stopped grinning. He didn't actually think she *had* gone commando, but that hadn't stopped his imagination working overtime last night.

Or this morning in the shower.

In fact, it worked overtime all day. Not even the hard grind of practice managed to erase it, much to the chagrin of Griff, who was less than impressed with Tanner's sudden inability to hold onto the ball.

"What the fuck?" he demanded as Tanner dropped the ball for the fifth time. "Are you all right there? You need to go and have a bit of a lie down? A massage? Rub some more pretty lotion into those hands of yours? How about a one-way ticket to the goddamn bench?"

"Sorry, Griff." Tanner grimaced, aware of the other guys watching the byplay. "Distracted."

Griff just looked more pissed off at the admission. "Since when do *you* get distracted?"

Tanner's focus was legendary. He didn't *do* distraction. Especially where women were concerned. When he got on that field, his concentration was always absolute. There hadn't been a woman yet who'd messed with that.

"Hot date with that journo last night, coach," Linc explained helpfully.

Tanner hadn't told any of them about going out with Tilly, so Linc had to have found out via Twitter.

"Oh, Jesus." Griff shook his head. "Please tell me you *did not* sleep with the Standard journo? You're supposed to be making things better, not *fucking* things up."

Tanner shoved his hands on his hips, affronted at the suggestion. "I did *not* sleep with her. Just because Linc is a walking hard-on, doesn't mean we all are."

"That's Mr. Walking-Hard-On to you." Linc grinned.

"Fuck off, Linc," Griff growled before he turned his attention back to Tanner. "Get your head in the game. I swear to God, captain or no captain, I'll bench your ass."

Tanner believed him. Griff would defend his players from outside attack with his last breath, but that didn't mean he thought they all farted rose petals. He was old school. Tough love was his motto.

Tanner was still thinking about Tilly's *bare* ass when he opened the Standard on Friday morning. By the time he was done reading the article, he didn't know whether to laugh or put that ass over his knee and spank it.

He hadn't known what to expect but it hadn't been this.

It wasn't an open attack on him. It was a skilfully written piece chronicling his early years and the birth of his generous celebrity. The suits in the offices would be most satisfied. But he still felt the subtle bite of it—the hint that beyond the facade was a flashy egotist.

Tanner Stone's celebrity is burning bright, his ego burning even brighter. Let's hope his almost childish delight in throwing his sizeable reputation around isn't compensation for a lack of size in other departments.

She'd seen right through his attempts to dazzle her with his fame. To impress her. The posh restaurant, the autographs, the posing for pictures, the lobster, the tickets he'd given to the maître d for his string pulling.

And she'd implied he had a small dick.

He'd laughed about that. If there was anyone on the face of this planet who knew what he was packing, it was Matilda frickin' Kent.

He hadn't meant to come across as an ego-tripping celebrity. He'd just wanted to show her how far he'd come. That he wasn't just the boofhead footballer he'd been in high school. That he was more refined now. Worthy of a Stanford graduate.

Worthy of her.

Posh restaurants. Exquisite food. A private balcony. Deferential treatment. Women were supposed to love that shit, right?

But that had been his mistake. He should have known better than to lump her in with everyone else. Tilly wasn't like other women.

She never had been.

She'd never cared much for money or status. She'd cared about the intangibles. Heart and soul. Gut. Kindness. Integrity. Strength—of character, not of body.

Fine. Challenge accepted.

Tanner shut the paper with renewed determination. Tilly's article might have put a lesser man off, but not him. He resolved to try again. Try harder. He wanted another shot with her—in fact, it was fast becoming an obsession, and he was willing to do whatever it took.

He just needed to show her a different side.

He grabbed his phone and dialled the work number printed on her card. She picked up on the third ring.

"Hello. Matilda Kent speaking."

"'Perhaps his almost childish delight in throwing his sizeable reputation around,'" Tanner quoted, "'is compensation for a lack of size in other departments...' You might have warned me you were going to be mean."

He deliberately kept his voice smooth and low. He might have been obtuse about some things on Tuesday night, but he hadn't been oblivious to her physical response—the way her eyes had drifted closed when he'd touched her face, the ragged hitch to her breath.

There was a slight pause. "Can't handle the truth?"

He laughed. "I tackle guys three times your size for a living. I can handle *whatever* you throw at me."

"So you're up for another meet?"

Tanner grinned. "I was born up, baby."

"Really, Tanner? Are you going to turn *everything* into a sexual innuendo?"

"Hey, you started it by questioning the size of my junk."

He could almost hear her eyes rolling. "That's going to get *really* tedious."

"Are you saying I'm boring? Because according to Twitter, it might be love."

"Oh, yeah. That's where I go to for *all* my relationship advice."

Her sarcasm dripped through the phone. "Hey, rugbybunny1 is rarely wrong."

"And what about slickstonesmistress?"

Tanner suppressed the urge to gloat. She'd been following the Twitter conversation. "What about her?"

"*Is* she?"

Tanner frowned. "My mistress?" He laughed. "I've never met the woman. She could be an eighty-year-old granny in outer Kazakhstan for all I know."

"But you like it, right?"

If she was digging for more dirt on his ego, Tanner wasn't playing. "Well, I prefer her Twitter handle to slicksucksdicks."

She laughed. It huffed out as if it had taken her by surprise, like someone had snuck up behind her and squeezed her hard.

"Thought you'd like that one."

"Hellz yeah, I'm following that one for sure."

Tanner smiled. Her genuine delight was a massive turn-on. "So, where should we go on our next date?"

"*Interview,* Tanner. Interview."

"Right." Tanner hadn't even realised he'd said date. But that's what it was as far as he was concerned.

She could call it whatever she damn well wanted.

But where did you take a woman who ordered risotto—hot soggy rice as far as he was concerned—when there was lobster?

"I can do better, Tilly, but I'm racking my brains, here. You're a hard woman to impress. I'd forgotten that about you."

"Maybe you shouldn't try so hard."

Tanner knew a piece of good advice when it was wrapped up in a bow. "Okay. Fine. What would make your heart beat a little faster?"

"If you're thinking skydiving, forget it. I don't see the point in jumping out of a perfectly decent plane."

Of course. Tilly was completely down-to-earth. She'd

been raised by a grandmother who believed in keeping both feet firmly on the ground…and doing good works.

Aha! That was the way to Tilly's heart.

"I'm thinking Monday night. Seven o'clock. The Chapel in Kings Cross. There's a soup kitchen there. There's always a mound of washing up to do and plenty of time to chat."

Silence greeted him. Clearly she hadn't been expecting that. "Yes. Okay." More awkward silence. "But don't forget to call the paparazzi. I'd hate for you to miss a photo op."

Tanner grinned as the phone went dead in his ear. Tilly had claws.

He couldn't wait to feel them down his back.

Chapter Five

Matilda was running a little late for her interview with Tanner. The crosstown traffic, always awful at this hour, had been compounded by an afternoon storm that had brought down trees and messed with traffic lights. Unfortunately, it hadn't done much to relieve the stifling humidity. Remnants of the storm rumbled and sizzled in the heavy clouds overhead as Matilda stepped around a puddle in her low-heeled sling-backs.

She hoped it wasn't some kind of portent. The electricity between her and Tanner the other night had been more than enough to contend with.

Welcoming lamps outside the old chapel ahead gave the weathered stone a warm glow, and Matilda picked up her pace, aware of the damp cling of her shirt and the limp plaster of her hair to her forehead. She felt as if she was wading through a wet sponge.

She hadn't expected Tanner to choose a soup kitchen, and she was still puzzling over it. The fact that she wasn't able to get his measure was a huge puzzle. She'd always been able to tell where he was at.

But her article—written deliberately to annoy him—seemed to have just rolled off his back. She didn't understand. Most of the men she knew would be furious to be publically called on their shit. But not Tanner. He'd just laughed down the phone and told her he'd do better.

And then asked her what would make her heart beat faster.

If only he knew how fast her heart had been beating in that lift the other night, and in those seconds she'd thought he was going to kiss her, he wouldn't have asked at all.

She needed to keep that shit to herself. She was on a mission here to reveal to the world their rugby darling was a giant ass. She wasn't going to let his confusing flirting—or *Twitter*—derail her objectives.

Matilda reached the gate and hurried down the potholed path, dodging more puddles as she headed for the stairs to the left, which led to the basement soup kitchen. The Chapel had been running a meals for the homeless programme, staffed entirely by volunteers, for the better part of three decades.

It was a Kings Cross icon.

She slapped a hand against the warped and peeling white door and pushed it open. Several long tables were filled with people eating, from ancient-looking men and women right through to hollow-faced street kids and bewildered families.

The low murmur of voices instantly cut out at her arrival and Tanner, who was sitting with a bunch of old guys at a table toward the back looked up from his conversation. She guessed she stuck out like a pimple on a pumpkin in her pencil skirt, silky red blouse and heels. Not to mention the impractical sheer black, thigh-high, lace-topped stockings she was test-driving for her column on the latest in fashion tights.

Her choice of clothing had been fine for the fridge-like conditions of a city office block, or maybe even a hot date, but not the kind that involved crippling humidity and some heavy duty washing up.

Her plan had been to nip home and change after work, but the storm had put the kybosh on that.

"Aha," Tanner exclaimed into the silence, rising to his feet.

He was in dark blue jeans and a white T-shirt with the Sydney Smoke logo over one firm pec, leaving a good few inches of his half sleeve of tats visible. Matilda swore every female gaze in the room swung and fixed on him. Even a little girl with dark ringlets and a raggedy-ass doll glanced up from her food and smiled at him.

"Didn't I tell you she was cute as a button, gentlemen?"

There were several enthusiastic nods and grins, and one, "I wouldn't kick her out of my cardboard box," followed by laughter.

Matilda blinked at the sooty-faced man who grinned a gappy smile in her direction.

"Ignore him," said a woman with steely grey hair and a warm Irish brogue. She was wearing a religious collar with her plain grey civilian blouse, and a dainty gold cross around her neck. She smiled at Matilda as she approached. "Homeless humour."

"Gotta laugh at something when you refuse to serve booze," the same man grouched.

"We're not a bar, Eric," she chided with a sparkle in her eyes.

"More's the pity," he muttered.

"Hiya," the woman said, extending her hand. "I'm Sister Kathleen. I'm running the show tonight. You must be Tilly? Thanks so much for your help."

Matilda's smile faltered a little as she shook the other woman's hand and glared at Tanner bringing up the rear. "Matilda," she corrected politely.

Conversation started up again as Tanner reached them. "I'll show her the ropes, Kathleen."

The nun nodded and smiled the most serene smile Matilda had ever seen. She looked like nothing would ever bother her. The same could not be said for Matilda as Tanner slid a hand under her elbow.

She was officially pretty damn bothered as his warm, sweet aniseed scent invaded her nostrils and intoxicated her senses. He smelled good enough to eat, like he'd been sprinkled with ouzo and dusted with sugar.

She wasn't sure if she wanted a shot glass or some kind of straw for snorting.

"The dishes await," he said cheerfully, ushering her toward the kitchen.

Her heart skipped a beat as the heat from his body and the sizzle from his touch combined for a particularly potent double whammy. Matilda plastered a smile on her face as she pulled out of his grasp. "Lead on," she murmured.

He didn't argue, and she followed him through a set of swinging doors behind the serving area into the stiflingly hot kitchen. With the door and windows shut, the sub-street level room still held the heat from several large industrial ovens.

"You wanna wash or dry?" Tanner asked as he strode over and opened the door that led out to a stairwell accessing the alley above. He reached up and flipped several levers connected to the bank of high louvers that opened directly onto street level.

The air stirred marginally. But it was better than nothing.

Matilda glanced at what seemed to be a hundred pots, pans, and roasting dishes crusted in hard black globules of food that looked incinerated in place.

"Jesus. Do they use a flamethrower to cook them?"

"I think the ovens are old and temperamental."

"Or ex crematorium stock."

He laughed. "I'll wash. Looks like brute strength is required."

Matilda wasn't about to argue. Might as well put those ridiculous muscles to good use. "I doubt I could write them into submission somehow."

"No," Tanner agreed, heading to the sink and flicking on the taps, intent on filling the industrial-size sink, and agitating the water as he squirted in some detergent. "You *could,* however, write about how I heroically and uncomplainingly scrubbed pots for hours while being witty and charming all at the service of some of the city's less fortunate."

"You want me to add how woodland animals came in from the alley to befriend you?"

He grinned. "As long as there are serenading bluebirds."

Matilda tried very hard not to respond to his easy teasing. The man obviously remembered her weakness for old-school Disney animations. *That* sure as hell made her heart *beat a little faster*.

"Is that why we're here?" she asked, picking up a clean tea towel from the pile near the sink, trying not to stand too close. She used to find their height disparity funny and kooky, and they'd often laughed about it. Now it was plain disturbing.

In all the *good* ways.

"So, I can see the man who eats lobster also has a social conscience?"

She glanced at him in time to see the tightening in the angle of his jaw. "You seem to know me so well," he said lightly, obviously keeping his temper in check as he dumped the first lot of dishes into the water. "Why don't you tell me?"

Matilda shook her head, pulling back on her hostility. She didn't even know where it came from. After eight years, she should have been over all this crap. But scratch the surface, and there it was.

Simmering away.

"Not any more I don't. I used to always know what you were thinking."

She mentally kicked herself as soon as the words were out. It sounded wistful and kind of sad, and she didn't want him thinking she sat around all day yearning for yesterday.

Those days were long gone. *Dead* and gone.

Thankfully he laughed, throwing his head back, clearly finding something very funny. "Well, that wouldn't have been hard," he said. "Rugby and boobs were pretty much it."

Boobs. Something she'd lacked. Which Jessica Duffy hadn't.

She looked down at her A cups. *Still* lacked. They were doing their best to look present in one of those magic push-up bras, but they were never going to win a wet T-shirt contest.

She glanced up to find him staring at them, too. Her nipples ruched into hard points at his blatant interest, and Matilda cursed the humidity that plastered the usually loose fabric of her blouse to said nipples.

She folded her arms across her chest. "Eyes front, Tanner."

"Sorry." He held his hands up in fake surrender, not looking remotely sorry at all. "You shouldn't mention boobs if you don't want me to look at them."

"*I* didn't."

"Oh, yeah. Sorry. Habit."

"*Bad* habit."

"Aren't those the best kinds?" He grinned.

Matilda rolled her eyes as Tanner returned his attention to the sudsy water and what his hands were doing, not what her nipples were up to.

Time to change the subject. "How are your family?"

"Good," he said. "Mum and Dad are still up north. Dad's retired. Mum's still really involved in the school even though none of us are there anymore, and the rugby club. I want them to come to Sydney but they love it too much up there."

Tanner came from a small town in a whole other state, a few thousand kilometres north of Sydney. He'd been identified early as having talent and had been given a scholarship to attend the prestigious rugby academy that Matilda's inner Sydney school was known for.

"And your sisters?"

"Kel's backpacking around Europe. Meggsie's working on a fishing trawler in the gulf, and Rails is studying criminology in Townsville."

"Wow," Matilda said, impressed. "Go them." Eight years ago, they'd all been in primary school.

"What about your grandmother?" he asked. "Still attending protest meetings?"

Matilda smiled. "Hell yes. The day she doesn't want to paint a sign for a march or write a letter to the local politician for some cause or other is the day she'll lie down and die."

As a kid growing up, the nice people in the neighbourhood had called her grandmother eccentric. Others had called her plain old crazy. But Hannah Kent was neither. She was someone who believed in justice and a fair go for everyone, and couldn't bear it when some missed out.

Matilda knew people thought her gran was odd, but it had never occurred to Matilda to be embarrassed by her. It was her grandmother who'd stepped into the void after her mother had died when Matilda had been two weeks old. And a year after that, when her son, Matilda's father, had taken his own life.

She owed her grandmother everything. Her loyalty most of all.

"Do you think she'd like tickets to see the Smoke play?"

Matilda laughed. "Unless you want a lecture on the evils of corrupt sporting officials, and how much third world hunger could be wiped out if big money sport fell off the side of the planet, I wouldn't suggest it."

He grinned. "Thanks for the tip."

He pulled a large pot out of the water and gave it a quick squirt with a retractable rinsing hose that was fitted with a trigger nozzle. It had gone in looking like something from Chernobyl and had come out pretty clean. He placed it on the drainer. "I liked your gran."

"Yeah," Matilda said, picking it up. "She knew."

She'd liked Tanner, too. Gran had always asserted that a man with sisters was a good catch. But damned if Matilda was telling him that when they were standing side by side, their arms occasionally brushing.

Tanner laughed. "Was I that transparent?"

The question clawed at her. Hadn't they both been transparent? Young and in love like nothing could ever tear them apart?

"Enough of that now," she said, determined to drag the conversation in a safer direction. "I'm supposed to be interviewing you." She pulled her Dictaphone out of her bag, pressed record and sat it on the low ledge formed by the splashback, a reasonable distance from the water.

"Fire away," he said, his biceps flexing as he scrubbed at the bottom of a baking dish. "Ask me anything."

It was on the tip of her tongue to ask why the fuck he'd cheated her on that night. Had it been just the kiss, or had it gone further after Matilda had run from the party?

It sure as hell looked like that's where it had been heading.

That question had haunted Matilda for a long time. After all, it was no secret that Jessica had wanted Tanner, and why would he resist her perky DDs when he'd already dealt his relationship with Matilda a fatal blow?

But they were hardly questions pertinent to her feature article. And she really had to stop letting it matter. Wouldn't Jessica *mean-girl* Duffy just love to know she was still screwing with Matilda eight years down the track?

She had to stop giving her nemesis that kind of power.

"You wanna pick up where we left off?" she asked.

He glanced at her, a smile turning his mouth wicked, mischief dancing in his impossibly blue eyes. "You mean last week, right?"

"Yes, Tanner. *Last week*."

He chuckled. "Can't blame a guy for trying."

She shot him a don't-mess-with-me look. "Don't bet on it."

He didn't appear remotely chastised as he turned his attention back to the dishes and picked his life story up again. He talked pretty much non-stop over the next hour as they tackled the mountain of washing up that just seemed to grow as diners came and went.

Kathleen bustled in and out, bringing in plates and crockery as they were used, along with the large metallic dishes where food was kept warm as it was served. Tanner, who appeared to know Kathleen quite well, teased and flirted outrageously with the older woman, who indulged him far too much for Matilda's liking.

"Enough of your blarney there, Slick, or I'm going to have to insist you volunteer every time I'm rostered here," she said cheerfully.

"I don't think you're supposed to monopolise volunteers."

"Psshhff," Kathleen grunted waving her hand dismissively. "I'm in charge of the roster and you're good for my ego. Plus you're not too shabby to look at. Don't you agree, Matilda?"

Matilda wasn't sure nuns were supposed to notice such things, but even so, "not too shabby," was putting it mildly. "If you like that kind of thing," she shrugged nonchalantly.

She'd be damned if she was going to puff his ego up any further.

He chuckled as Kathleen quirked an eyebrow at him and said, "I wouldn't be getting her to write your biography."

By the time the dishes were finally done, Tanner had chronicled his journey from France until joining the Smoke, and Matilda was a pool of sweat. Her blouse had succumbed to the moisture from her damp skin, clinging even more efficiently. The feathery tips of her hair had long ago lost the will to wisp.

Tanner, on the other hand, looked fresh as a freaking daisy. How could he smell so good when she was so…sticky?

He smelled like…liquorice allsorts.

God, yes, *that* was the spicy-sweet aroma she'd been trying to place all night.

Great. Now he really *was* good enough to eat.

"Man." She threw the almost soaked tea towel on the bench and fluffed the damp, limp strands of hair off the back of her neck as she tried to blow her equally damp fringe off her forehead. "I think I've completely melted away."

She pulled at the front of her blouse and fanned it in and out to try and relieve some of the stickiness. It was times like this she was grateful she had no cleavage.

"Put the fan on," Tanner said, as he wiped around the sink with a washcloth.

Matilda blinked. "There's a *fan?*"

"Sure. Just inside the store cupboard."

Matilda's legs followed the direction of Tanner's finger to discover the storeroom and the fan just inside the door. She turned to him as she hauled it out. "Could you not have told me this before now?" she asked incredulously. "Did you not notice I was a dripping mess?"

"You told me to keep my eyes forward."

Muttering to herself, Matilda carried it to the closest power outlet, which was on the bench opposite. She set it down on the gleaming metallic surface, next to another large sink, quickly plugging it in, turning it on, and pushing the button that said *High.*

She dragged it close to the edge and positioned herself right in front of it, bending forward slightly so the breeze was directed straight down her top, grabbing the bench on either side with both hands. She shut her eyes with a low moan as the powerful breeze ruffled her blouse, instantly cooling the sweat and evaporating the stickiness of her skin.

She only wished she could straddle the damn thing and have it blow straight up her skirt. It was kinda heated up there, too.

Unfortunately, she couldn't blame that one on stockings and humidity alone. Tanner Stone in those jeans and tats was responsible for most of the heat between her legs.

"Better?" he asked from somewhere behind her.

She could hear the thick streak of amusement in his voice even above the racket of the fan.

"So, *so* good," she confirmed. "Better than an orgasm."

Tanner's dick responded predictably to her choice of words. The visual stimulation of her ass wiggling as she rocked from foot to foot and weaved her torso in front of the fan, didn't help things.

Better than an orgasm?

Clearly the woman was having lousy orgasms.

Another long, low moan came from her direction, hardening his dick to granite. She obviously wasn't the only one who needed to cool down. "Would you like me to leave you two alone?"

Although, that was the last thing his dick wanted. It was settling in for the show, and Tanner wasn't about to disappoint a particular part of his anatomy that had never once let him down. He couldn't even say that about his kicking foot.

She didn't answer, so Tanner assumed she either hadn't

heard, or she wasn't going to dignify his innuendo with a comment. Knowing Tilly it was probably the latter.

He lounged against the bench, his feet crossed at the ankles and arms folded across his chest. He knew he should just walk away and leave her and the appliance to it. But not even an advancing All Blacks haka could have dragged him away from the swing of her ass.

A loud clap of thunder echoed through the louvers and open door. "God, I wish it'd just rain already," she grouched, angling her head from side to side, the tips of her fine blonde hair fluffing out with the breeze. "Something has to cool it down out there."

Out there? If something didn't cool it down in here, he was going to walk up behind her and bend her over that damn bench.

She wanted rain? He glanced to his left. He could give her rain.

Flicking the tap on, he reached for the rinsing hose, pulling it out of its receptacle. Before he could change his mind, he aimed it at her back and squeezed the trigger. A jet of cold water shot from the end and hit her right between the shoulders.

Chapter Six

Tanner released the trigger at her audible gasp and the violent arching of her back. She whipped around to glare at him, the fan blowing the wisps of her hair forward. "What the fuck, Tanner?"

With the light behind her, she looked like a furious punk-rock angel. Her outrage was funny as hell, and he couldn't help but laugh. "Oh, I'm sorry. Did I make you wet?"

Air shunted noisily in and out of her chest as she gaped at him, obviously speechless. But Tanner knew that wouldn't last for long.

"It takes a lot more than a hose to make me wet."

There it was. *Atta girl, Tilly.* "I remember."

Her brow furrowed, and she opened her mouth to let fly, but he didn't give her a chance. He squeezed the trigger again, the water hitting her right between her breasts, soaking her blouse.

"Tanner *Stone*," she half squealed, half gurgled as she raised her hands, trying to block the spray, averting her face.

He released the trigger, and the water cut out. Slowly she

turned her face, dropping her arms as she glanced at the front of her blouse. He looked, too. He couldn't stop. The red fabric was plastered nicely to the slight swell of her breasts.

He remembered how much she'd hated her A cups. But he also remembered how perfect they'd been—small, yes, but perky and crowned with the palest of pink nipples.

And now? They looked as sweet as he remembered.

Sweeter.

Slowly, she returned her gaze to his. "This blouse," she said, the whiskey flecks in her eyes glowing like fire in opals, her nostrils flaring, "is a warm-water wash only."

"I can add in some hot," he suggested, reaching for the tap again.

"Don't"—she held up a finger to halt his movements—"even think it. Drop it, this instant."

A loud clap of thunder underpinned her warning.

It was on the tip of his tongue to say *make me*. But he'd probably already pushed her far enough for one day. "Okay, fine," he sighed, turning and placing the rinse hose back in its receptacle.

He didn't expect the cold slap of water between his shoulder blades, and gasped at the shock of it, whirling around as it seeped into his T-shirt and ran down his back.

"Oops. Sorry," she said, the hose from the other sink in her hands.

She was pointing it at him like a weapon, her arm extended, her finger hovering over the trigger. She looked like one of those chick television detectives in their skirts and heels, looking glamorous and powerful and sexy with their guns out.

She was totally hot right now.

A Mona Lisa smile played on her lips as her chest rose and fell, her gaze darting all around, a wariness to her stance and a tenseness to her muscles, primed for his next move, primed to react. Possibly to flee.

Clever woman.

"So that's how it's going to be, huh?" He reached for his hose again, but she didn't give him the chance, shooting a stream of water at his chest this time, as he had done to her.

"Oops, sorry," she repeated. "Guess I have a bit of a trigger finger going on."

The water was bliss on his heated skin, especially with the breeze from the fan, but it was doing nothing to cool Tanner's engines. His heart banged against his ribs as anticipation tightened his belly and his balls.

She wanted to spar with him? *Bring it on.*

Tanner cocked an eyebrow. "You sure you want to get any wetter?"

She cocked her eyebrow back at him before lowering the hose and aiming it at his fly. "Big talk for a man with no weapon."

His dick did not respond as if it were under imminent threat. *Oh, no.* It was practically busting out of his pants, begging for it. "I think I can hold my own."

A massive boom of thunder rattled the pots and pans hanging from a nearby rack, just as she squeezed the trigger.

"Doesn't look like," she said, water soaking the front of his jeans. His dick got harder at her cockiness. "Oh, dear…" She dropped her gaze. "that could be difficult to explain."

He chuckled and Tilly smiled at him, triumph replacing wariness. *Rookie move.*

He lunged, the kind of move that had earned him a formidable reputation on a football field. She let out a tiny squeal and tried to twist away, but she was too late. He wrestled control of the hose from her easily, wrapping her up in his arms, whipping her around to hold her captive, her front trapped against the bench.

The fan blew on them directly, cooling nothing down as

she struggled against him, her ass taunting his groin. His arms banded together around her ribs locking her arms by her sides, hemming them in with the thick muscles of his biceps. The nozzle of the hose came to rest just under her breasts.

He was aware of the frantic expansion and retraction of her rib cage, the erratic pull of her breath. As erratic as his own.

"Let me go," she said, her voice husky.

"Just trying to cool you down, baby," he taunted.

"It's not working," she argued.

"Maybe this will."

Tanner squeezed the trigger gently, sending a brief spurt of water straight into her cleavage and up her neck. It spread south as well, further soaking her blouse and wetting his forearms.

She gasped, her arms struggling against the bands of his again, her ass pushing backward.

"How's that?" He smiled.

"What do you think?"

"Not working for you?" he asked innocently. "How about this?"

Holding her steady with one arm, he slid the other down her belly, pushing the nozzle into the waistband of her skirt.

"*Tanner*," she squeaked. "Don't you *dare*."

Tanner chuckled as he squeezed the nozzle. *Oh, he dared, all right.*

"Sorry 'bout that," he said as she gasped and spluttered, wiggling her ass *so damn good* as she desperately tried to back away from the spray. He pulled the nozzle out of her skirt. "Guess I have a bit of a trigger finger going on there," he mimicked, thoroughly enjoying himself.

Enjoying the feel of their bodies together again. The sharp intake of her breath. The way he fit around her, the back of her head cradled against a pec. The rub of her ass.

"Okay fine," she said, the fight suddenly leaching from her body. "You win. Just put the damn hose away and let me go."

Tanner chuckled, loosening his arms as he threw the hose back in the sink. He didn't try to reclaim his previous position, instead placing that hand on the bench near her hip, his other hand sliding to the countertop on the opposite side. The fronts of his thighs were still pressed into the backs of hers. His groin still trapped her hips to the bench, but not like they had when she was struggling.

He waited for her to push him away, tensed for a sharp elbow to the abs now that he wasn't restraining her. But there wasn't one. Just another crack of thunder reverberating around the kitchen.

He didn't know what her placidness meant, exactly, but he sure as shit was going to exploit it for as long as she'd let him. He'd dreamed of being this close to her since he'd first seen her again in the locker room, wearing that awful pantsuit. Wild horses couldn't have dragged him away.

From his height vantage, he could see the fan blowing cool air on her wet blouse. See her eyes shut as if she was enjoying the light caress. See the pebbling of her nipples.

Were they hard because of the cool water and the artificial breeze? Or for other reasons? The same reason his dick was hard?

Was she as turned on as him? His instincts told him yes but…he couldn't tell with her anymore.

The urge to slide his hands onto her belly and rip all her buttons open roared through him with a primitive insistency, and he curled his fingers around the edge of the bench so he wouldn't. He didn't want to do anything that might startle her out of whatever trance she was in.

She angled her head to the side. Was it to catch the breeze on her neck or did she want him to nuzzle her there?

"That feels better, doesn't it?" he murmured, lowering his head to the vicinity of her ear, her hair brushing his cheek.

More thunder rumbled in through the open door, pressing in and thickening the air.

She didn't say anything.

"You look much cooler."

"Uh huh," she murmured, her voice as thick as the air around them.

Tanner wasn't. Tanner was about to burst into frickin' flames. He brushed his lips against the exposed side of her neck, his heart thundering in his chest, his dick so hard she must be able to feel it jammed against her ass even through several layers of fabric.

"Tanner don't," she whispered, but it was weak. Not very convincing.

He nuzzled lower. "Don't what?"

"Kiss me."

It was more a pant this time as she settled herself more firmly against him, her hand creeping up around his neck, anchoring where hair met nape, her fingers furrowing into the shagginess of his hair. Tanner shut his eyes as the sensation streaked straight to his balls and almost brought him to his knees. He locked his legs hard.

Okay, she didn't want him to kiss her? Fine. As captain of the Smoke he often had to change tactics on the fly. He could sure as hell do that here. He dropped his hands to her hips. To that damn skirt that had been driving him crazy all night. Thunder rumbled as if in warning but he paid absolutely no heed.

"I like this skirt," he said, keeping his voice low and right near her ear as his hands slid down the sides. "Makes a guy wonder just how to get a girl out of it."

He walked his fingers along the seams, drawing fabric up as he went, inching the skirt higher. "Do I undo the zip or do I just" — his fingers kept gathering fabric, slowly, surely — "ruck it up at the sides?"

She huffed out a shaky half-laugh. "Well, you're the expert on rucking."

He smiled, his lips brushing the tip of her ear. "Damn straight I am."

Tanner didn't care, as the skirt eased higher on her thighs, that they were in a soup kitchen. He didn't care that Kathleen, or anyone else for that matter, could come through the door at any moment. He was beyond caring that Griff would probably bench him for the entire season if he knew where Tanner's hands were right now.

All he cared about, as the rain finally crashed down with furious intensity, was the sensuality of her silky stockings, the eroticism of their lacy tops and the illicit thrill as his hands hit bare skin.

She tensed and gasped as his hands slid around to the fronts of her thighs and he groaned, "*Jesus, Tilly,*" directly into her ear to be heard above the pelt of rain. The aroma of rain and shampoo and the way she'd always smelled in that sweet spot just behind her ear joined the hammer in his chest and the roar in his head.

She moaned, low and needy, turning in his arms as if she knew the pressing enormity of *his* need. Like he was going to die if he didn't kiss her right this second. She didn't talk, she didn't even really look at him, just at his mouth as she slid her hands around his neck, raised herself up on her tippy-toes and yanked on his neck.

Tanner didn't need any more encouragement, meeting her mouth halfway, their lips clashing with an intensity to rival the storm. His hands, thanks to his earlier ministrations with her skirt, slid onto the cheeks of her nearly exposed ass, and he dragged her in close and tight, lifting her a little so he could grind the hard press of his dick against the almost exposed apex of her thighs.

The kiss was wild and out of control as he strained to breathe, forgot to think. Their heads twisting, their mouths devouring, their tongues hunting. Tilly—*his Tilly*, her taste, her smell—filled up every breath until Tanner was dizzy with it. The imperative to *possess* her echoed in every frantic beat of his pulse.

And then the back door slammed.

Hard.

A huge clap of thunder and a massive gust of wind crashed the flimsy wood back into its frame, and Tilly wrenched her mouth away, looking around wildly as if she was coming out of a trance, confused about where she was.

Who she was with.

"*Fuck,* Tanner," she swore, pushing him back and slipping out of reach, walking away. He barely registered the flash of butt cheek attached to a petite leg and a sexy, lace-topped stocking before she was yanking her skirt down.

Tanner shoved a hand through his hair. "Tilly, I—"

She whirled on her heel, holding up her hand to silence him, the fingers of her other hand pressed to her mouth as if she was still confused as to how Tanner's lips had ended up on hers.

The rain on the roof roared around them as they stood, breathing hard, staring at each other.

"I told you I didn't want you to kiss me," she said, her tone accusatory.

"I seem to remember it was you who kissed me."

She glared at him, but Tanner didn't care. Whatever had happened just now had been completely mutual. If she wanted to bury her head in the sand about whatever it was that was still there between them, then she could go right ahead, but he wasn't going to be her enabler.

She lifted her chin. "It wasn't even very good."

Tanner knew a bald-faced lie when he heard it. She'd been as affected by the kiss as he had. Hell, she was still breathing hard, the pulse in her throat still rapid, her eyes still a little glazed. "You tell yourself whatever gets you through the night, Tilly."

Her brows knitted together as she opened her mouth to say something, but somebody bustled in from the dining room and she shut it with a snap. "Oh, fabulous," Kathleen enthused, oblivious to the tension. "I see you're all done then?"

Tanner, his back to her, dragged his chaotic thoughts together to mumble a vague, affirmative reply.

"You can both go when you're ready, with a blessing and thanks from everyone here at the Chapel," she prattled on, moving closer to Tanner and Matilda. "I hope you brought your brollies, though. It's chucking it down out—"

Kathleen stopped as she finally got close enough to take both of them in. She looked at Tanner's white T-shirt, transparent in its soaked state, and the big wet patch on Tilly's skirt. She glanced at the puddles on the floor then back at them, an eyebrow raised. "I was going to say be sure not to get wet out there but I see that's kind of moot."

"I'm sorry about the floor," Tilly said, her cheeks pink. "I'll mop it up."

"I'll do it," Tanner said testily, annoyed that Tilly couldn't even look at him.

Tilly didn't argue. But she still didn't glance his way, either. "Thanks," she mumbled before thanking Kathleen, too, and declaring she had to run. She'd scooped up her belongings and disappeared out the back door in record time.

"You're losing your touch there, Slick," Kathleen said, as she stared after Matilda.

"What makes you say that?"

"I may be a woman of God, but even I know the Good Lord invented much more interesting ways of getting a woman wet."

Tanner had given up being shocked by Kathleen. The nun had worked the rough streets of Sydney half of her life. She could talk smack with the best of them. His best option was to ignore her, which he did as he headed for where the mop was stored.

Unfortunately, Kathleen wasn't done yet. "I like her." Tanner clanked around in the store cupboard. "She's the one."

Tanner rolled his eyes. "I suppose the *Good Lord*"— Tanner pronounced it with an Irish brogue—"told you that, did He?"

"Hell no," Kathleen grinned. "You just did." She inspected him for a moment then gave a firm nod. "It'll do you good to chase after someone who's running for a change. Women come far too easily for the likes of you."

And on that divine announcement, she swept out of the kitchen, leaving Tanner to mopping and wistful thoughts of easy women.

• • •

Matilda went home, every cell of her body seething with the taste and smell and *audacity* of Tanner Stone.

How *dare* he take advantage of her temporary insanity like that? How dare he wet her and wrestle her and wrap himself around her and slide her skirt up and kiss her neck and make her so damn crazy she could barely think?

Since when had she become some kind of amnesiac nympho around him?

It was the charm that did it. That had lulled her into a false sense of security. The way he was with Kathleen and the men from the shelter. And how he'd talked about his parents and his sisters and *her grandmother*. The stories he'd told about his early days in rugby and the anecdotes about his teammates.

Yep, Tanner Stone oozed charm from every pore. It had lowered her defences around him. And it couldn't happen again.

She had a goal here—revenge. And she couldn't lose sight of it.

Still hyped up from the kiss, Matilda sat down at her laptop and wrote her feature article in under an hour, steaming along, getting it all out before the outrage died down and she had to face the facts about her own part in that kiss tonight. About the lie she'd told.

It wasn't even very good.

It was a wonder she hadn't been struck down dead considering she'd been standing in a freaking chapel in the midst of a massive electrical storm with a *nun* nearby.

But Tanner had seen right through her.

You tell yourself whatever gets you through the night, Tilly.

And he'd been right. She'd had to tell herself *something* because the kiss had shaken her to the core. And not just physically, although if the door hadn't slammed shut, Matilda was pretty sure they'd have gone for it right there in the Chapel's soup kitchen.

Something which probably would have earned her a one-way ticket to hell.

Right. Like she hadn't already been on a fast track to purgatory since the day of the locker room and Tanner's low-slung towel. She'd been having some seriously vivid flashbacks about what was behind that towel, memories that had been confirmed today as the hard ridge of his erection had ground between her legs. Her skirt, rucked up to her freaking armpits, had been no protection.

But it hadn't just been how his body had made her body feel. She could do something about that—physical relief was easy, after all. She had Thor and Zeus—her toyfriends—to see to that, and for damn sure one of them would be coming out tonight.

It was the unfurling of something inside her that was more than physical—a memory long since shrunken and closed in on itself after Tanner's betrayal. But it was blossoming now, reminding her of their connection, of the intimacy of their shared history. Of how he used to make her feel. How he'd touched her.

On an emotional level.

And that was dangerous. Because she wasn't about to throw herself in front of the Tanner Stone train again. *Never* again. The definition of stupid was doing something over and over and expecting a different result.

Matilda Kent had won a scholarship to Stanford University. She didn't do stupid.

So she applied her big brain to the article instead. Ostensibly, she continued Tanner's rugby journey, careful not to openly criticise, choosing instead to damn him with faint praise all while exposing him as the charming *player* he was.

For anyone with two X chromosomes, Tanner Stone and his extraordinary superpower should come with a warning label. What is this power you ask? Charm. Yes, charm. Nuns, toddlers, homeless people, and little old grannies alike fall under his spell. Be sure to stock up on your kryptonite panties if you're heading to a game.

Chapter Seven

Tanner laughed out loud on Friday morning reading Tilly's column. *Kryptonite panties?* He was *never* going to live that one down.

He checked his Twitter stream, which seemed even more amused by Tilly's kryptonite quip than he was.

rugbybunny1—Methinks @MatildaK wants @slickstone to get into her #kryptonitepanties #sydneysmoke #holysmoke #mightbelove

slickstonesmistress—@slickstone can get into my #kryptonitepanties whenever he wants #SuperSlick #holysmoke #mightbelove

madforrugby—I'ddropmy#kryptonitepantiesfor @slickstone #SuperSlick #holysmoke #mightbelove nottherealtannerstone—Calling all designers: #kryptonitepanties stat for my fans please #holysmoke #mightbelove

And from someone called superheroesaremyweakness

Word from Kryptonian elders. Disapprove of #kryptonitepanties #lethalweapon #holysmoke #mightbelove

This time Tanner didn't resist the urge to play along.

.@MatildaK was obviously wearing #kryptonitepanties when she did a runner Mon nite. Help me out tweeps. Put in a good word 4 me? #mightbelove

He hesitated over the "mightbelove" hashtag before sending the tweet out into the ether. But he liked its flirtiness, and he knew his Twitter base would go crazy over his adoption of it.

And hell, as far as he was concerned, it might very well be love.

Predictably, there was an avalanche of tweets extolling his virtues directed at Tilly, from the cute to the downright filthy. Tanner laughed as he read them on his way to the stadium for practise. He pictured Tilly getting madder and madder as they hijacked her Twitter stream—her brow furrowed, her cheeks pink, her lips pursed. Just like she'd been Monday night when she'd pulled away from him, her mouth still wet from his, uttering that dirty word.

Fuck, Tanner.

She was obviously not goaded sufficiently this morning, though, to join in the Twitter conversation.

Most of the guys were in the locker room when Tanner

entered. "Oh, look," a bare-assed Dex observed in that slow, measured way of his. "It's a bird."

"No." Bodie shook his head. "It's a plane."

"Nah," Linc grinned, "it's Superman."

"Hope we all brought our kryptonite panties, fellas." Donovan added.

Tanner had been right about never hearing the end of it. "Bite me," he said as he headed for his locker, ignoring the good-natured jeers.

He laughed when he reached his destination to find a Superman shield with its big red *S* had been cut out and stuck with electrical tape to the front of his locker. He pulled it off with a grin, crumpling it in his hand.

"That's me," he confirmed. "Ten foot tall and bulletproof. Now—" He hauled his T-shirt off over his head. "Let's go kick training ass."

• • •

By the time Tanner returned to their locker room three hours later, it was fair to say that training had kicked his ass. And, judging by the far less jovial mood around him, he wasn't alone. Griff had run them ragged, wanting them all primed for their match tomorrow night. It was only early in the season, but Griff hated to lose.

And Tanner had let him down again. Sure, he hadn't fumbled any balls this time, but his head still wasn't one hundred percent in the game. Maybe Griff hadn't noticed, but Tanner sure as hell had. His attention had wandered far too often to a pair of pebbled nipples and a strip of silky skin above a black lacy edge.

He reached for his phone and checked Twitter. The hundreds of notifications were just what he needed to put a smile back on his face. Twitter was on his side, and Tilly still hadn't bitten.

He tapped out another quick tweet.

Coach not too happy about my ruined concentration during training session. I blame you @MatildaK #mightbelove

By the time he'd stripped off his sweaty clothes and kicked out of his footy boots, the tweets and retweets were coming thick and fast.

Hey @MatildaK put @slickstone out of his misery #mightbelove.

Go on @MatildaK you know you want to #mightbelove

If #sydneysmoke loses tomorrow night we blame you @MatildaK #mightbelove

Tanner grinned as he hit the shower. His work here was done.

• • •

Matilda was over anything to do with Tanner Stone by their Sunday lunch date. Her Twitter stream had lit up since the article and Tanner's provocative tweet. If she had to read about one more of his virtues, she was shutting her account down for good.

She'd told herself to ignore them, but her colleagues at the office had taken great delight in stopping by to read them. Aloud.

Most were witty in the way only one hundred and forty

characters and no requirement for punctuation engendered. A lot were eagerly whipping up speculation with the new hashtag #TannMat. Even the mightbelove hashtag had been mentioned by Callie Williams, a notorious gossip columnist at a rival paper.

Most were encouraging, clearly enjoying the whiff of a fresh celebrity romance. Some were not so nice—creepy, twisted, bordering on offensive. Matilda hadn't blocked or unfollowed so many trolls in a long time.

At least the Smoke had won yesterday. Matilda wasn't sure the mood on Twitter would have been so convivial if the team had lost. Thanks to Tanner, she'd have probably been booed off the social media platform.

But at least she felt on solid ground today as she drove to their third date.

Interview. Fuck. *Interview*.

Damn Tanner and his continual insistence on calling them dates.

He'd texted last night to ask if they could meet at her grandmother's so he could catch up with her, and Matilda had agreed with alacrity, inviting him for lunch the next day.

A Sunday roast at gran's was part of Matilda's routine, and having Tanner on *her* turf was a welcome change. He wouldn't dare try anything there. Hannah Kent would flay him alive with the sharpness of her tongue alone if he so much as put a toe out of line.

She may have had a soft spot for Matilda's high school boyfriend, but Hannah had always insisted that Matilda and Tanner respect her rules and not fool around in the house. He'd been banned from her bedroom and not allowed in the house if Hannah hadn't been there.

And Tanner had followed her rules to the letter, earning a great deal of Hannah's respect. Although there was that one time out back behind the shed when things had gotten a little carried away... They'd been sent out to pick some tomatoes and peas from the garden for tea, but somehow Matilda had ended up with her hand down his pants, urging him to forget Hannah's rules, so desperate to feel him inside her that a quick fuck against the shed wall had been all she'd been able to think about.

Luckily, he'd pulled them back from the brink. But it had been a close call. And after Matilda had gone in he'd had to hang around for a while outside waiting for his giant erection to subside.

He'd phoned her later that night complaining about his bicycle ride home with blue balls, and she'd taken pity on him and told him exactly what she'd wanted to do to him behind the shed as he'd masturbated, coming in a long, loud growl that had made her feel like the most powerful seventeen-year-old on earth.

Matilda smiled, thinking about it now as she pulled up in front of the home her grandmother had lived in ever since she'd married over sixty years ago. The smile died as a car pulled in behind her. It was some kind of dual cab, four-wheel drive thingy. It didn't look particularly new or flashy, but it was still a long way from his second-hand bike.

She'd bet blue balls weren't a problem in it.

Hell, she doubted blue balls were a problem for him at all these days.

Matilda's face heated up, and she shook her head as she watched him in her rear view mirror getting out of his car. *Idiot.* Do *not* think about his balls. Be they blue, black, or bright orange with polka dots.

The last thing she wanted was pink cheeks when she greeted him. It was going to be embarrassing enough to face him given what had happened the last time they'd been together.

But they were on her turf now. *Her* turf. And Gran would

be there for her.

He knocked on her window, and Matilda startled, her pulse accelerating, although she wasn't entirely sure it had anything to do with the knock. She glanced at him, noticing the bright bunch of flowers in his hands for the first time. "Are we going in?" he asked.

"Yep." She nodded, making a great show of unbuckling her seat belt and gathering her handbag, hoping the activity gave her pulse a chance to settle and the warmth some time to dissipate from her face.

He stood back as she opened the door and climbed out.

"You look lovely," he said, taking in her cool maxi halter dress that crisscrossed at her nonexistent cleavage and fell to her ankles.

He leaned down to kiss her again like he had that first time, briefly on each cheek. The light aroma of roses, the heavy scent of lilies, and the faint whiff of liquorice intoxicated her, and she swayed toward him briefly, her eyes closing before he pulled back and her lashes fluttered open again.

"Ladies first," he said, gesturing for her to precede him through the gate.

Matilda's legs were decidedly unsteady as she navigated the front path and the three cement stairs to the door. It was locked, as usual, but she used her key, calling out as she pushed it open.

"Gran?"

"Through here, girlie."

Her grandmother's affectionate name for her always made Matilda smile, and they followed the still strong voice and the mouth-watering smell of cooking meat into the kitchen to discover her almost eighty-year-old grandmother perched precariously up a foot ladder, trying to reach the smoke detector.

"*Gran!*"

"Mrs. Kent," Tanner said, dumping the flowers on the dining table as he strode over to the ladder, anchoring his foot and hands on it immediately. "I don't think it's very safe to be doing that."

Hannah Kent smiled down at Tanner. "Hello, my dear boy. So nice to see you again. How long's it been?"

He chuckled. "Too long. Now how about you let me do that?"

Hannah got one of those recalcitrant looks Matilda knew too well. The kind that always shocked police officers at demonstrations, who mistook her stooped frame and grey hair for a sign of gentility. "Do I look like an invalid to you?"

"Absolutely not, Mrs. K. But you wouldn't want to see me emasculated in front of Matilda, would you?"

Hannah laughed her great big hooting laugh, running her gaze over Tanner's broad shoulders. "Tanner Stone, you could dress up in drag and still not be emasculated."

Matilda blinked. *Dress up in drag?*

"Fine, have at it," she said, climbing down from the ladder, handing him a battery. "Sick of the damn thing chirping at me. Although I'm not sure if it's this one or any of the others."

Tanner took the battery. "I can change them all if you like. It's no bother."

"That'd be fabulous," Hannah beamed at him.

Matilda grabbed her grandmother's hand as she took the last step down. Hannah gave her a noisy kiss on the cheek but was distracted by Tanner heading up the ladder. Frankly, so was Matilda, and they both looked their fill. The tail of his checked, collared shirt hid that spectacular ass from view, and a pair of chinos that ended just above his knee concealed his powerful thighs, but the hard knots of his smooth calf muscles were on open display and, fortunately for them, now at eye level.

There was no leg hair, and Matilda realised belatedly that

he must wax. It wasn't unusual—a lot of athletes at the elite level did—she was just surprised to find it so damn sexy.

Her grandmother leaned in and brought her lips close to Matilda's ear. "Please tell me you're tapping that," she whispered.

Matilda swivelled her head to stare at her grandmother. *Tapping that?* What the fuck?

Her grandmother hooted at Matilda's consternation. "What?" she whispered, clearly unperturbed. "I keep up with the lingo."

Matilda didn't even know where to start. Should she explain that it would be Tanner who was doing the tapping if tapping was what was happening, which it *definitely was not.*

Nor would it be, either.

"Where's the next one?" Tanner asked, climbing down, apparently blissfully ignorant of the conversation.

"The hallway and in my bedroom," Hannah smiled at him and handed him another two batteries off the table. He smiled back and picked up the stepladder, heading for the hallway.

"I take it that's a no?" her grandmother asked as Tanner disappeared from sight.

Heat flushed Matilda's cheeks. She'd never told her grandmother what had happened with her and Tanner. Just that it had been a mutual decision, given she was going to Stanford and he was going to buttfuck nowhere. Hannah had thought it very wise and sensible.

Matilda wondered if her grandmother would be so gung-ho with the *tapping* if she knew about Jessica Duffy.

"I'm *interviewing* him," Matilda said, keeping her voice low.

Hannah snorted. "You're a journalist, girlie, not a doctor. You haven't taken the Hippocratic oath."

"It's one of those unwritten laws. Professional ethics. Integrity." Matilda folded her arms. "You know, that thing you drummed into me."

"So I did." She shook her head and tsked. "That was silly of me. Integrity hasn't given me any great-grandbabies yet, has it? I'm not getting any younger, you know."

"I thought you wanted me to be a career woman?"

"I do. A career woman with babies. And you two would make very nice babies. Did you see those calves?"

Her grandmother bustled over to the oven to check the meat just as Tanner entered the kitchen. Matilda, still gaping over the whole baby thing, hoped like hell he hadn't heard it.

"That smells great, Mrs. K," he said.

"It's roast pork. You're favourite, I seem to remember."

Matilda rolled her eyes. "Oh, please. Tanner liked everything you made."

"I remember," she beamed.

"Your lasagne," Tanner agreed. "Your vanilla slice. Those caramel milkshakes you used to make us after school for an energy boost."

"Oh, yes," Hannah laughed. "But I don't really think it was my milkshakes that was bringing you to the yard, was it?"

There was a moment of stunned silence, and then Tanner burst out laughing, his hand splayed over his flat belly.

"*Gran!*" she chastised, shooting an annoyed glance at Tanner.

"What?" Hannah dismissed in good humour. "You're not teenagers anymore, dear. Don't have to mind my p's and q's these days."

Tanner managed to wrangle himself back under control. "Was I that transparent, Mrs. K?"

"Of course, sweetie." She beamed. "Now, this is probably twenty minutes away from being done. Would you like a beer?"

Matilda barely registered the flow of conversation after that, as Tanner and her grandmother caught up on old times, bantering over roast pork while she tried to regain her balance. This wasn't the way it was supposed to pan out. This was *her* turf. She was supposed to feel in control here. But with her grandmother practically pimping her out to Tanner in the hopes of great-grandbabies, Matilda felt all at sea.

Frankly, she was relieved to be shooed outside after lunch to sit on the small undercover porch with Tanner while her grandmother made them cups of tea. That was until she spied the old shed standing where it always had, in pretty good shape considering how old it was.

Tanner, who was standing at the wooden balustrade, looking out over Hannah's still extensive veggie garden, turned suddenly. "I remember that shed," he said, a smile playing on his wicked mouth and creasing his sexy face, emphasising the broken angle of his nose.

Matilda was pleased she'd already taken a chair as her legs trembled and her belly looped the loop. She set her gaze on the row of snow peas creeping all over a wire frame in the middle of the garden, as her cheeks flamed. She couldn't have held his gaze even if she'd wanted to, now the state of his balls and how they'd relieved them all those years ago was back front and centre.

"Looks like you do, too," he grinned.

Grinned like the thing that ended their relationship hadn't happened. How could he act as if the good times were all there were between them, and not be ashamed at what he'd done?

Had she really meant that little to him?

They could have gone on to have so many more of those times. Hell, maybe they could still have been together.

Matilda took a couple of deep breaths, determined to bury the kernel of hurt that pulsed inside her. She cleared her throat to change the subject, but then Tanner lounged against the top rail and almost toppled off the patio into the cement-edged petunia bed below when the balustrade gave away.

"*Tanner!*" Matilda's pulse leaped as she sprang out of her chair, reaching for him as he flailed for a beat or two before grabbing the nearby post and righting himself. "Are you all right?" she gasped as she grabbed his arm.

"Yes," he assured her, looking behind him. It was only about a foot drop, but Matilda supposed when you were one of the highest paid rugby players in the country, any potential for injury was to be avoided at all costs.

Hannah wandered out with a tray as Tanner crouched down to inspect the damage to the railing. "Oh, dear," she said, putting the tray down. "That's been a bit wobbly for a while now."

"Gran, why didn't you tell me? I could have got someone around to get it fixed."

Dear God, what if Gran had fallen into the garden bed? She could have broken her hip or smacked her head and be lying there for days, seeing as how she refused to wear the medical-alert device Matilda had purchased for her.

"I'm perfectly capable of making my own arrangements, thank you, girlie. I even bought some paint a few months back to give it a bit of a facelift, but I rarely sit out here these days, so it always slips my mind."

"No worries," Tanner said, standing. "The wood's rotted all the way along, though. But that's easily replaced. Can't be more than a few meters. Have you got a tape measure?"

"Only a seamstress one. Not the retractable ones that builders have."

"That'll do," he assured her.

Matilda blinked as her grandmother went off in search of one. "What are you doing?"

"I noticed a hardware store just down the road. I can buy the materials and have the railing replaced in a few hours."

"You…can?"

"Sure," he grinned. "I juggled rugby and part-time work as a carpenter for a couple of years before I joined the pros. Had to support myself somehow."

"Oh." Matilda had assumed he'd been paid well all along. "You didn't mention it."

He shrugged. "You didn't ask."

It hadn't been said with any kind of accusation but it felt like one. He was right, she hadn't asked. It was easier for her to look upon him as a guy who had everything rather than the boy who'd come from nothing.

Matilda resolved to be more thorough, as Hannah arrived back with the tape measure. Tanner completed the measuring efficiently. "I'll be back in about half an hour and have this done in no time," he said to Hannah, who grinned at him like he'd offered to build her a whole new house. He glanced at Matilda, a small smile playing around his mouth. "You wanna come for a ride?"

"Of course she does," Hannah piped up.

Matilda frowned at her grandmother. "No. Thank you. I'll wait here and keep Gran company."

He grinned. "Suit yourself." Then he nodded at them both and departed.

Her grandmother sighed and shook her head at Matilda. "I remember a time when you would have jumped at that invitation."

Her grandmother was right. Hell, if Tanner had owned a car instead of a bike they'd have probably lost their virginities much, much earlier.

Matilda shrugged. "It's complicated."

Hannah inspected her face for long moments. "Life's short, sweetie. I sure as hell don't have to tell you that."

She got a familiar distant look on her face and Matilda knew her grandmother was thinking about her own losses. Her daughter-in-law who'd died shortly after Matilda's birth, her son who had taken his life at the age of twenty-five, and her beloved husband who had died of a heart attack at forty.

"Grab on tight to those you love and never let them go," she said, patting Matilda on the arm as she shuffled past.

Matilda watched her grandmother disappear inside before turning to face the back yard and that damn shed. Did she still want Tanner as fiercely as she had that day?

Absolutely.

But sex wasn't love. No matter how much her grandmother wanted it to be so.

Chapter Eight

As good as his word, Tanner was back in half an hour with not just pre-fabricated railings and balustrading but a bunch of different shiny new tools as well—a hammer, a drill, a nail gun, a spirit level, a builders tape measure, and assorted screws and nails. Just under three hours later, Hannah was in possession of a brand spanking new wooden railing that looked sturdy enough to last another sixty-odd years.

Matilda was incredibly touched. Tanner Stone, elite rugby player, worshipped by men and women alike all around the country, who could have been anywhere today celebrating his team's win yesterday, had knuckled down like an ordinary Joe and fixed her grandmother's porch.

It was pretty damn hard to stay mad at a man who was being so damn sweet.

"Now, where's that paint?" he asked Hannah.

"Tanner," Matilda protested. "You don't have to paint it as well." It was getting close to five and they'd already monopolised his company long enough.

Not to mention the acute case of horniess she was coming

down with at the sight of Tanner wielding a power drill and a nail gun.

"It's in the shed," Hannah supplied, clearly not worried about monopolising Tanner's time. In fact, she'd bent his ear about one thing or another the entire afternoon while plying him with cold drinks and insisting Matilda act as his lackey.

Pushing her closer and closer to Tanner and his tools.

"It's no bother," he said, grinning at Hannah. "There's still a good couple of hours of sunlight. Should be able to get that first coat on, anyway, especially if Tilly helps." He cocked an eyebrow at her. "Whaddya reckon? Many hands and all that stuff, and you can interview me as we go."

Matilda hesitated, but it seemed churlish to not be willing to paint her own grandmother's porch railing. "Okay...sure."

Hannah took him down to the shed and the two of them disappeared for a couple of minutes before reappearing with some paint cans and brushes. Tanner set them down on the patio as Hannah kept going into the house. He used a screwdriver to pry the lids off.

"She wants the railing this federation green colour and the balustrading white." He handed Matilda a brush and the green paint. "You do the hand rail. I'll tackle the uprights."

Hannah re-joined them, carrying an old button up shirt. "Here, sweetie," she said to Matilda, "this will protect your dress." She glanced at Tanner. "I'm afraid I don't have anything big enough for you."

"No worries," Tanner said, lifting his arms and yanking up the shirt from the back, pulling it over his head without removing the buttons, and tossing it on the nearby chair. "I'll just go without."

Matilda's mouth ran dry as her gaze devoured the hard smoothness of his chest and abs, the breadth of his shoulders, and the meaty bulk of biceps decorated in green inky thorns. Daily training session had honed the body of his youth into that of a man.

A very fit man.

Hannah winked at her granddaughter. "I'll leave you two to it. The gardening show's on the telly now, and I hate to miss it."

Matilda tore her gaze from Tanner's frame to glare at her grandmother's retreating back. She knew for a fact her grandmother hated the gardening show.

She shoved her arms through the old shirt and did up the buttons with fingers that trembled uselessly. How the fuck was she going to concentrate on painting when all she really wanted to do was take that brush to his body?

"Have you got your recorder thingy?" he asked as he sat at the far end of the porch.

Did she? Matilda thought hard through a haze of lusty thoughts. Yes, in her bag. "It's inside," she said. "I'll just go grab it."

As soon as she was safely in the house, Matilda sagged against the wall and prayed for strength. And it wasn't just about his body, although God knew it was hard enough to resist when he was fully clothed. What was even more dangerous was the mellowing of her antipathy after his work here today. If she started to thaw on that front, it would be just a short, slippery slope to his arms.

And she didn't want to be another in his conga line of women. She wasn't someone who could separate sex from a relationship—especially not where Tanner was concerned.

He'd move on and she'd be *screwed*.

And not in the good way.

Thirty minutes later, she'd successfully managed to ignore the flash of wide shoulders in her peripheral vision as she asked Tanner questions about his early days with the Smoke whilst simultaneously creating a work of art that could have been displayed in the Louvre. She'd painstakingly painted the curved surface, taking her time, knowing that sooner or later she and Tanner were going to be meeting somewhere in the middle as he worked his way toward her from his end and then she'd no longer be able to ignore him.

And that time was now. They were close enough so that his elbow occasionally brushed her leg.

"Swap you," he said, placing his paint can out of reach as he rose easily to his feet, towering over her all of a sudden, his shoulders and chest a big block of muscle dazzling her gaze.

Beneath the harsh chemical smell of paint, she caught a warm undertone of ouzo. He was so close that if she wanted, she could reach out and touch him. Hell, with her head where it was, she could just lean in and lick a nipple. They were right there, two to choose from, flat and brown, with the steady thump of his heart beating between them.

Matilda dragged in a breath, her own heart beating double as she forced herself to take a step back, to look up into his eyes. Neither of them said anything for long moments, just stared at each other like they couldn't get enough.

"You have some paint on your face," he said finally, his voice deep and low like the purr of a jungle cat.

It was just what Matilda needed. "I do? Where?" She'd been careful, but paint did have a habit of splashing. She raised the back of her wrist to her face, rubbing first one cheek then the other. "Has it gone?"

He shook his head. "You missed a spot," he said, dabbing his paintbrush against her nose. Matilda gasped as she automatically rubbed at it.

"And here, too," he said, smiling this time as he painted a stripe down the side of her neck.

Matilda reared back, trying to avoid another swipe of

the paintbrush down the bare flat of her forearm, almost succeeding as she grabbed the railing behind her.

"Shit," she swore, as wet paint greeted her. She brought her hands up to inspect the damage, then, holding them out to him, showed him his handiwork. "This is *your* fault." She glanced at her handprints on the rail. "And I'm going to have to repaint that."

He had the gall to laugh. "No way, dirty girl. You grabbed the rail all by yourself."

The way he said *dirty* tipped the situation into dangerous territory. The protest died on her lips as something dark and illicit tugged at her throat and thickened her breath.

She dragged in some air as the broad span of his shoulders taunted her. "You mean like this?"

Matilda grabbed his chest, slapping both palms flat on his pecs, smearing green paint all over them, grinding deliberately hard over his nipples, watching her handiwork with fascination, conscious of the catch in *his* breath.

"There," she announced, wiping her hands down his abs before finally dropping them to her sides. "That's better."

He looked down at himself, and Matilda followed suit, taking great satisfaction in the pattern of the dark green smear. Her gaze snagged on his nipples and the way the paint had stained them a darker shade of brown. The illicit thrill of a moment ago returned, and she salivated as the urge to suck them clean rode her hard.

Would his breath hitch if she did?

Would it drag a moan from his throat, so temptingly close?

But, no. That would be crazy. Not to mention possibly detrimental to her health. She flicked her gaze to his, hoping he couldn't read her mind. Then he'd know just how dirty this girl really was.

His mouth kicked up on one side. "I guess I deserved

that."

Matilda smiled sweetly. "*Fucking A,* you did."

And somehow it broke the ice. They crossed over positions and went back to their painting, but there was an ease between them now. It felt more like they were having a conversation instead of an interview as the topics switched back and forth from rugby to her job and Hannah's antics over the years.

Hell, Matilda even found herself laughing. And that wasn't so natural given how badly she still wanted to lick his chest clean.

Once they were done, Tanner put the paint away and they cleaned the brushes and themselves off with turpentine he'd found in the shed.

Hannah joined them, nodding approvingly at their handiwork. "Are you available for some nailing at Matilda's tonight, Tanner?"

Matilda, who was pouring some turps into her hands, overshot badly at the blatantly provocative question. It splashed all down the front of her maxi dress, soaking in.

"*Gran!*"

The acrid turpentine smell filled her nostrils and Matilda prayed she didn't spontaneously combust from embarrassment right at this moment. She'd go up like a freaking torch.

"What?" her grandmother asked with an air of innocence that no one who knew Hannah Kent would ever fall for.

"I'm up for some nailing," Tanner said, shooting an indulgent smile Hannah's way, his voice deep and warm with laughter.

Despite herself, an answering smile lit Matilda's face.

"It's just that she has all this artwork in her apartment that she brought back from the U.S. and had framed, but still hasn't gotten around to hanging."

Matilda glared at her grandmother as a different kind

of hanging came to mind. "It's fine." She dismissed the suggestion. "They're on my to-do list. I'll get round to it one day."

"But he's here, and he has the tools," Hannah went on undeterred. "And he's offering. Aren't you Tanner?"

Tanner responded dutifully to the prompt. "Most definitely."

"So you should be gracious enough to accept."

"Really, it's fine," Tanner reiterated. "Have hammer" — he picked it up and winked at Matilda — "will nail."

"It's settled then," Hannah said, smiling triumphantly, like she'd negotiated a peace deal in the Middle East rather than Tanner banging some nails into a wall.

Or, as her grandmother clearly saw it, banging Matilda *against* a wall.

But Matilda knew to choose her battles, so she smiled serenely and made noises about going as Tanner threw his shirt back on over his head. Hannah looked disappointed that the show was over but Matilda was relieved to finally have the temptation removed.

"I'll arrange for someone to come and pick up the old wood tomorrow," Tanner said as Hannah saw them both to the front door.

"Thank you, Tanner. It's been so lovely to see you again. Girlie, you make sure you bring him back soon."

Matilda rolled her eyes. No way was she encouraging the old biddy. "Good night, Gran," she said and pecked her cheek.

Hannah waved them off, calling out, "Don't do anything I wouldn't do," before closing the front door.

Tanner's sexy chuckle followed her all the way to the cars. "See you at your place?" he said, as he opened the car door for her.

Matilda shook her head. "Honestly, don't worry about it. She'll never know, and I won't tell her."

Tanner quirked an eyebrow. "Really? You going to take that risk? I seem to remember she has eyes everywhere."

Matilda remembered, too. Her grandmother had always seemed to know where they'd been and what they'd been up to. "We're twenty-six, Tanner. I'm prepared to risk it."

"You know I'm just going to follow you to your apartment anyway, right?"

Matilda sighed. *Of course he was.* "Fine."

"Might as well surrender to the"—he grinned and held up the hammer—"inevitable nailing."

Matilda shook her head. "You're as bad as she is."

"What if I promise to be good?"

"You mean come in, hang some art, then leave again?"

"Yup." He raised the hand with the hammer and set it against his chest like he was taking the pledge of allegiance. "Cross my heart and hope to die."

One half of Matilda was throwing up flashing yellow warning signs. But the other half remembered his incredible kindness today at her grandmother's and urged her cut him some slack. He had the tools and the time. And he'd offered.

Not to mention the nagging she'd cop from her grandmother if she didn't give in.

"Fine," she sighed. "But the only nailing going on tonight involves my painting, *capisce*?"

"*Capisce.*"

She would have felt better had he not followed it with a dirty sounding chuckle.

Twenty minutes later, they'd survived the agonisingly slow lift ride, and Matilda was ushering Tanner into her apartment. It was a modest two-bedroom set up bought with the assistance of the small inheritance she'd received from her parents' estate, which her grandmother had kept in trust until she'd returned from Stanford.

Unfortunately, this being Sydney, where the property market had been burning hot for the last decade, she'd had to supplement it with a mortgage that was bound to keep her in servitude for the next twenty-five years.

"This is great," Tanner said, looking around the open-plan kitchen, dining, and lounge area with its eight-foot ceilings.

He looked great, somehow instantly at home in her apartment, his hammer in one hand, a spirit level in the other, the bulk of his frame not diminished by the high ceilings. Often, with just herself for company, the apartment felt empty, but not with Tanner filling up the space.

"I have a feeling living on the harbour at Woolloomooloo is probably nicer."

He shrugged like it didn't really matter to him at all. "I have a faster lift."

Matilda snorted. "I should bloody hope so."

"That them?" he asked, nodding in the direction of the half dozen frames stacked together against the far wall.

Matilda nodded, grateful that he was being all matter-of-fact and efficient, sticking to his word—get in, bang in some nails, hang some art, get out.

He strode over and separated them, then crouched down and inspected each of the one-meter square watercolours. "Nice," he said appreciatively. "Do they have some kind of personal meaning?"

"A friend I roomed with painted them. They're different aspects of the Stanford campus."

"Oh." A strange kind of stillness settled over him. "It looks great." But his voice was flatter now.

"It was. It…is."

"You pleased you went?" he asked, still staring at the paintings.

Matilda remembered how she'd been all set to turn down the scholarship and follow Tanner on his journey. Just as well she'd found out about his predilection to infidelity in the nick of time.

The turmoil of that time reached right into the present day and wrapped its hands around her gut. Her mellowing attitude toward him hardened again as a familiar ache took up residence in the middle of her chest. It seemed important in this moment to show him she'd had no regrets about walking away from him.

She raised her chin. "Best decision of my life."

He nodded, slowly. "Good." He dragged his gaze off the watercolours, pushing to his feet, all efficiency again. "Where do you want them?"

Matilda felt absurdly like crying. Or fleeing. He could have been here for the last five years. They could have made a home together. She'd managed to forget the pain of their history this afternoon, or at least the full force of it, but it was back with a vengeance. Matilda's hand trembled as she pointed to the expanse of wall behind her television. "I thought in two rows of three. They're numbered one through six so…in order left to right?"

He pulled his newly acquired tape measure out of his pocket as he strode over to the wall, planting the end of the retractable tape on the floor and running it vertically up the wall to a point about a foot above his head.

"About this height for the top row?" he asked, not turning around.

Matilda sucked in a breath, her lungs filling with the chemical fumes of turpentine still lingering in her clothes. "Whatever looks good," she said dismissively. She needed to get away from him doing manly things in her apartment and the sudden crippling sensation of loss, of what could have been. "Do you mind starting without me? I really need a shower. I smell like a chemical factory."

"Go ahead," he said, measuring horizontally now, obviously preoccupied enough not to make some quip about joining her or coming to scrub her back.

Matilda fled to her room on unsteady legs. She sank down onto her bed when she was close enough, sucking in chemical-laden breaths as the ache beneath her sternum grew bigger. This was the kind of life she'd always envisioned with Tanner. Living together. Marrying at some point. Having kids.

Over the years she'd told herself it didn't matter. That she'd find that connection with someone else. But she hadn't been able to let a man close enough emotionally after Tanner's betrayal. And that had been fine, too. She wasn't the kind of woman who felt her life was over because she didn't have a guy in it.

Until tonight. Until Tanner was walking around in her apartment with his tools, measuring her walls, being all handy, giving the space an overwhelming masculine air.

A maelstrom of anger, bitterness, and regret churned in her gut. He'd not only broken her heart eight years ago, but he'd stolen a future from her.

And that cut the deepest.

Chapter Nine

The shower helped. Or at least the time away from him to collect herself helped, as did the stern, silent lecture she'd delivered as she'd scrubbed away the turpentine. About no regrets. About looking forward, not back. About things happening for a reason.

Matilda heard hammering as she stepped out into the lounge area. The first two paintings on the top row had been hung and Tanner was banging in the third nail. He was standing on the low display cabinet that usually housed the television, which he'd moved to the floor.

It showcased his calves, and despite the heaviness of her emotional state, she totally checked them out. Again. The muscle definition was awesome, delineated perfectly, popping out from the back of his leg, big as grapefruits. They were clearly the powerhouses for Tanner's fearsome sprinting technique.

"That looks good," she said, walking toward him, determined not to betray her inner turmoil or how much his freaking *calves* affected her.

He looked over his shoulder, one of those easy smiles of his hovering on his mouth. It died pretty quickly, though, as his gaze took in her usual sleeping attire—loose silky boxer shorts and baggy T-shirt.

There was nothing sexy about what she wore to bed, which was one of the advantages of not having a guy in her life, and exactly why she hadn't thought twice about putting it on. But Tanner seemed to find her legs endlessly fascinating, and when he was done with them his gaze moved slowly north, zeroing in on her unfettered breasts, which he couldn't possibly know, as their meagre proportions were totally lost beneath her voluminous T-shirt.

Regardless, her nipples ruched into tight peaks, as if they were completely bare to him, and heat flared down deep and low. Maybe it was his even-more-than-usual height advantage? His gaze seemed extra intense towering over her like he was.

"You're wearing your glasses," he said, smiling suddenly, returning his attention to her face.

Matilda reached for them absently, the retro horn-rimmed frames that she knew suited the gamine features of her face. "Oh…yes." She usually took her contacts out and wore her glasses around home. Gran kept on about getting laser correction, but Matilda couldn't bear the thought of someone poking around with her eyes. "The turpentine fumes were irritating my contacts."

He dropped his gaze to her breasts again, and the heat coalescing in her pelvis pulsed between her legs and ran in molten rivulets like hot wax down her inner thighs.

"Cool shirt."

Matilda was relieved to glance down and give her neck a break. Bold black print proclaiming her to be "a superhero disguised as a reporter" stood out against the snowy white fabric.

She shrugged. "It was a present from Gran."

He laughed, and damned if her ovaries didn't twang a little. His gaze slid back to her face. "Of course."

Matilda desperately needed to claw back some control. Having him here all large and sexy in her apartment was confusing her resolve. She couldn't let her ovaries have *any* say in *any*thing.

They'd been Team Tanner since the locker room that first day.

"Shall I pass you number three?" she asked, not waiting for an answer, but stalking over to the opposite wall to pick it up and give herself time to get her shit together.

She took some deep, controlled breaths and headed back his way, handing it over, grateful when he took it and turned his attention to something other than her clothes.

An hour later, all the nails had been banged in, and the last painting had been hung. Tanner had been surprisingly thorough. He had been at Gran's today, too, but he seemed extra fussy here, making sure all the measurements were right so the paintings were all evenly spaced and level.

They chatted about Stanford as they'd worked, and the tension in Matilda eased as she talked a little about her time in the U.S. It really had been am amazing time in her life.

"Yup. They look straight to me," he said, his arms crossed as they both stood back a few feet on her shagpile rug and admired his work. "Whaddya reckon?"

Matilda angled her head from side to side, frowning. "I think the bottom middle is a little crooked."

He shook his head. "It's straight. The level doesn't lie."

"Yeah, but I reckon…" Matilda strode toward them, not breaking stride as she stepped up onto the low cabinet with relative ease to get a closer look. "I reckon this one definitely needs just a titch this way."

She fingered the bottom right-hand corner of the frame

and gave it a slight tap. The painting moved a whisker, and she leaned back a little to check the position. "That's better." She nodded, looking over her shoulder at him. "Don't you think?"

She caught his gaze on her legs before he switched his attention to the wall. He narrowed his eyes as he moved closer. "I think it needs to go over a little bit more."

Matilda turned quickly back to the painting as he pulled up about a foot behind and to one side of her. It was insane that she could be standing on a piece of furniture, a head above him for a change, and still feel dwarfed.

She was hyperaware of how close he was. He could reach out and touch her. If he wanted.

She gave the painting another tap to hide the leap in her pulse he'd caused with just his nearness. She went too far the other way, however, grimacing to herself as she switched sides and tried to compensate in the other direction.

"Yup, stop," he said. "I think that's it."

She stopped at his instruction, inspecting her work. It looked better, but she leaned back a little to be sure. She was too close, though, for an accurate assessment so she half turned to climb down from the cabinet. Unfortunately, she had her eye on the painting and not her feet, and she misjudged the edge.

She cried out, her heart rate spiking as her foot slipped and she pitched inelegantly sideways, flailing her arms as she went down, groping madly for some purchase.

She found it in the form of Tanner Stone.

"Tilly!"

Tanner reached for her as she toppled into his chest, her feet tangling with his, tripping them both up, her glasses flying off her face as they landed in a heap on her thick rug. The landing was a lot softer than it would have been had it been her hardwood floors, but it still knocked the breath out of her. And even if it hadn't, Tanner, who had done his best to avoid landing on her with his full weight, still added to the jolt. He ended up partially sprawled on top of her, half of his torso and one muscled thigh pinning her to the floor as they both lay in stunned silence for long moments.

Matilda hauled air into her lungs, staring at the ceiling, too winded to do anything other than try and breathe. Tanner, his forehead pressed into the rug beside her head, seemed to be having difficulty catching his breath, too. She didn't try to push him away or protest his position. She just lay there gradually recovering her ability to oxygenate her body.

It probably wasn't longer than ten or fifteen seconds before her breathing came easier, but that was soon secondary to other things. The solid wall of his chest. The hard heat of his thigh. The granite jut of his erection pressing into the bony crest of her hip.

Fuck. Matilda sucked in a ragged breath. He had a hard-on. *For her.* He was lying on top of her and he was…aroused. She could reach for him right now. Touch him. Reacquaint herself with that particular part of his anatomy.

Heat flooded her pelvis at the realisation, spreading south to tingle between her legs and burgeoning north to her breasts, her nipples hardening in their own blatant arousal.

Her heart thumped erratically—surely he could feel it? Every breath felt like soup, thick and laden with the scent of Tanner.

More *chemistry* than *chemical* now.

She remembered this. Her *body* remembered this. The glorious weight of him.

He'd always worried about how heavy he was compared to her but she'd revelled in the feel of him on top of her. The wild, feminine power of it. The sweet craving to feel his skin on hers. The drive to open up to him, to grant him possession, to take possession of him.

Apparently, as her heart practically punched out of her

chest, and her body melted to liquid beneath him, not much had changed.

He shifted slightly and Matilda stiffened, dragging herself back from the abyss. She should be pushing him away. She should be objecting instead of lying here wallowing in the long lost feel of him.

"Are you okay?" he asked, easing back, holding the weight of his torso off her.

Matilda's body lamented the absence, the urge to draw him down again a living, breathing demon on her shoulder. "Just a bit…winded."

He nodded but didn't move, his gaze drifting to her mouth then lower to her T-shirt. Her nipples were hard points against fabric that was now pulled taut against her, thanks to the fall. He stared for long moments, and Matilda's insides quivered as if he'd lowered his head to one and sucked.

She shut her eyes to block out the image. This was all kinds of madness. "*Tanner.*"

Matilda opened her eyes at the sound of her voice. It was deep and ragged, almost a growl. Maybe a plea.

"Tanner, what?" he asked, his voice as husky as hers as he flicked his gaze to her face. "Tanner, stop? Tanner, leave?" He slid a hand low on her stomach, the muscles beneath tensing in anticipation. "Tanner, touch me?" A lazy finger stroked the skin just above the waistband of her boxers, the sensation coursing white-hot need straight between her legs.

"Tell me what you want, Tilly," he murmured, his blue gaze earnest. "What you *really* want."

Matilda couldn't blame him for the confusion. She wasn't sure if she'd said his name as a deterrent or an encouragement. All she knew was he was hard for her and she wanted to touch him.

She shouldn't be feeling any of it. Wanting any of it. But she did. Her body remembered.

It *craved.*

She was at war with herself, her heartbeat pounding through her pulse points, roaring in her ears, driving lust and sex to every part of her body.

"This?" he demanded huskily, his hand finding the hem of her T-shirt and pushing under, sliding up her belly, coming to rest high on her rib cage, precariously close to a nipple screaming for attention.

Matilda sucked in a breath. "Tanner."

"This?" He dropped his mouth to her neck and nuzzled all the way down her throat. "This?" His voice was muffled as his tongue teased the hollow at the base of her throat and his hand slid the last inch or so to claim her breast.

Matilda gasped, her eyes fluttering shut and her back arching as his fingers clamped around her nipple. It wasn't painful, but it streaked like a burning arrow straight to her clit, hitting the target with an accuracy that stole the air from her lungs.

He was breathing hard when he lifted his head, his gaze roving her face, looking for God knew what.

Certainty? Permission? Surrender?

She didn't know if he found it, only that he groaned, "*Matilda*," all thick and needy, his control snapping, and he didn't ask her anything more, just pushed her shirt all the way up to her neck and swooped his head down to claim the nipple his fingers were torturing.

She arched her back again, still too stunned, too overwhelmed by the hot rush of lust to compute anything other than the pleasure coursing through her body. She didn't care that her breasts were too small, or that they were on her floor, or that she shouldn't be doing this.

With Tanner.

All she cared about was the hot suck of his mouth on her breast and the corresponding tug at her clit as if he was down there instead, as if there was a direct line from one to the other.

"*Christ*, you smell good," he groaned as he switched sides, and Matilda's whole body shuddered in response, muscles deep inside clenching and unclenching at the potent stimulus. His teeth grazed the hard tip and she cried out.

It hurt *so damn good*.

But then he was gone, her taut, wet nipples left to air dry as he headed down, tracing a wet path with his tongue, inching lower and lower, stopping to swirl around her belly button a few times before heading relentlessly south. He didn't even stop when he reached the band of her boxers. He simply tore them down, stripping them off her legs with his two big hands.

Matilda, who'd been somewhere out of her body, suddenly came back to it, her eyes flashing open, her head lifting to watch him as his hands spread her thighs, looking at her with complete carnal intent, his chest heaving in and out.

She was conscious of the fact that he was fully clothed and she was lying mostly naked spread before him. Conscious of the fact they'd never done this before. Not that he hadn't wanted to. He had. But at seventeen, Matilda had found it kinda gross and hadn't let him.

She hadn't understood why anyone would *want* to.

Thankfully, with maturity, she'd let other lovers take her further, and she was a fully paid up, card-carrying member of the cunnilingus club. And even though tongue action alone generally wasn't a consistent way to get her over the line, it felt fucking amazing and she never said no.

But she was acutely aware—shy even—that this was a first for them.

She needn't have worried, Tanner barely drew breath before he muttered, "Oh, yes," and settled himself between her legs, his tongue hitting the jackpot immediately.

"*Tanner!*"

With her clit already fully aroused from the nipple stimulation, it was excruciatingly sensitive. In fact, it was almost too much and she tried to buck and twist away from the relentless action of his tongue but he just clamped a big hand down on the stretch of skin between her hip bones and held her there, held her to his tongue.

"*Jesus,* Tilly," he groaned, lifting his head briefly. "You taste good."

And then he went back to it, his hands sliding to her nipples, lightly pinching and twisting their ruched peaks in time with every flick of his tongue against the hard nub of her clit, not deviating from his intent, not exploring anywhere else, just applying hard, unyielding pressure, both stimuli working in tandem to build her quickly, to push her over, ripples of pleasure swelling up from deep inside her belly, her buttocks, her thighs, pulsing hot and all-consuming from her clitoris, breaking over her in waves of intense release, ripping a cry from her throat and wringing the air from her lungs.

Matilda floated in a daze afterward, breathing erratically, her limbs too heavy to move. She was torn between melting into a puddle of quivering goo and apologising for how quickly she'd come.

No man had ever gotten her off that fast with his tongue.

He must think she was some sex-starved spinster, lying there like a bloody starfish, shattering uncontrollably at what was—in her experience—fairly minimal tongue action.

But neither melting or apologising were physically possible at the moment, so she concentrated instead on calming her tripping heart, dragging her body back to earth, and pulling the jumble of thoughts in her head back into some coherent sequence.

Tanner shifted and Matilda glanced at him. He was sat back on his haunches between her legs, looking pretty damn pleased with himself.

"I always knew that'd be fucking amazing with you."

The words were like a clap of thunder. Like a slamming door. The daze evaporated in an instant.

They *could* have been doing *this* for years. *He* could have been the one to introduce her to the delights of oral sex. Good, fast, *orgasmic* oral sex.

But he'd ruined it for them.

How dare he look so freaking *smug* like he'd just ticked an item off a sex list?

Going down on Matilda. Check.

Since when had sex become some kind of conquest for him? A series of goals to achieve rather than a statement of the heart?

And how dare he somehow make it sound like it was her fault that they hadn't been here before.

Hot stupid tears sprang to her eyes as she vaulted up, yanking her T-shirt down. She snagged her discarded boxers and underwear—should have taken her own advice and worn ones of the kryptonite variety—as she wriggled away from him, scrambling to her feet, shoving her legs into her boxers.

Tanner blinked as he watched the greased-lightning dressing display. Tilly's pants had gone on almost as quickly as he'd ripped them off.

Okay. Clearly he'd put his foot in it there. She was obviously mad, but he'd also seen a shine of moisture in her grey eyes. Hurting her had not been his purpose here tonight—quite the opposite. His dick deflated as quickly as it had sprung to life as he castigated himself for his choice of words.

He got warily to his feet. She was looking at a spot beyond his head, hugging herself, pulling her baggy shirt taut again, her glasses back in place. "Tilly, I didn't mean—"

"It's okay," she interrupted. "Just go, okay? Please."

Tanner frowned. He'd thought he was getting somewhere with her today. It had felt a little like old times at her grandmother's house. They'd laughed. He'd even go as far to say they'd had fun. And he'd loved listening to her talk about Stanford as they'd hung the paintings. He was so damn proud of her, and it made him happy to know that he'd made the right decision to sever their relationship.

And then she'd let him go down on her, when she'd *never* let him do that all those years ago. How many times had he fantasised about that, both during their time together and the years since? He could still taste her on his tongue, her scent still filled his head, and his heart beat faster just thinking about how fucking turned on he'd been.

Surely that in itself signalled a mellowing toward him? For Matilda to allow that particular intimacy, there must be something there?

And he'd just gone and cheapened it by bragging about his proficiency. Thrown it at her with a cocky *I told you so*.

Doofus.

He took a step toward her. "I think we need to talk, Tilly."

She shook her head, her eyes looking a little wild. "God, no, please…I'm fine, just *go*."

Tanner's ire stirred at her insipid word choice. *Fine?* She'd looked more than fine a few minutes ago. She'd been practically melted into the rug before he'd gone and opened his big trap.

He shoved his hands on his hips. "Is that it? You let me go down on you, and you come so loudly I'm pretty sure the cops are going to be kicking the door in any second, and now it's good-bye, see you later, don't let the door hit your ass on the way out?"

She shrugged, her expression bewildered. "You want some payback?" she snapped. "You want me to get on my knees and suck your dick?"

Tanner recoiled. "No!"

"Oh, you want a thank-you?" She gave a shrill laugh. "Thank you, Tanner. You are an oral sex god. I can do a hashtag for Twitter if you want. Hashtag gives great head or hashtag Captain Cunnilingus?"

Tanner stared, stunned for a moment. *Captain Cunnilingus*? It was so absurdly funny a laugh escaped before he could stifle it.

He would *never* live that one down.

"I'm sorry, Tilly," he said, grinning despite the absurdity of it all. "I don't want anything. I just want to…"

Love you.

His smile faded. His heart hammered in his chest. That's what he wanted. To love her again. But she didn't look in any kind of mood to be throwing that out there. He had some more making up to do. "I want it to be…okay between us again."

She stared at him for long moments, tears filling her eyes as she obviously struggled with what to say. Tanner wanted to go to her, to pull her into his arms, but he didn't want to scare her off saying whatever was causing that battle in her eyes.

She shook her head. "You don't get it, do you? You broke my *heart*, Tanner. And that's not okay. Things can never be *okay* between us again." She cleared her throat and blinked furiously, dissipating the tears. "You treated me like a fool, and you played with my heart, like it was one of your damn footballs to just kick around. But you fumbled the ball, Tanner, and you lost the game."

Her words may have been soft and calmly spoken, but they were as thorny as the tats on his arms. He hated seeing the hurt he'd caused. It was like thorns tearing into *his* heart. And even if he could have taken it back he wouldn't because she'd gone to Stanford and had a life. *Her life*. Not his. All he could do was go forward and hope that by doing so he could make up for what had happened in the past.

It was tempting to tell her the truth about that night, to clear his name. But now wasn't the time. She was too mad to hear it. She'd probably just reject it outright. But he wasn't going to pussyfoot around this anymore, either.

He wanted her back. And he was putting her on notice.

He took the two steps required to bring them within touching distance. He half expected her to take a step back, but she set her chin determinedly, obviously feeling stronger now she'd had her say.

"I may have lost," he said, lifting his hand and brushing a stray lock of fringe back into line, "but I'm older and wiser now, and my game's only gotten better. And I have three more dates—" He held up a hand as she opened her mouth. "*Interviews*, for a rematch. And this time I'm playing to win."

She didn't say anything, just held her ground, looking at him with her big blue-green eyes, so much bigger now with her wispy pixie haircut. If she was worried, she didn't show it.

But he heard the hitch in her breath as he walked away. And it gave him hope.

Chapter Ten

Somehow, Matilda wasn't sure how, she ended up on Tanner's arm ten days later, as his date to a black-tie charity thing for Farm Aid. At least, that was what every photographer and entertainment journalist on the red carpet seemed to think as he ushered her along.

As far as she was concerned, it was another interview opportunity. *Only.* No date. Definitely no Captain Cunnilingus. Although, God knew that had been running on a loop through her head ever since that night.

"Tanner!" Callie Williams, notorious gossip columnist, called him over. He sauntered toward her and her cameraman despite Matilda dragging her heels.

"Callie, how delightful to see you."

She beamed at him. "I see you've brought your Twitter amour with you."

Tanner smiled that cheeky grin of his. "We're old friends," he said, neither confirming nor denying anything about the state of their relationship.

Callie pouted. "Oh, go on. There's a lot of speculation

about you two. What about the 'might be love' hashtag?"

Tanner chuckled. "That wasn't started by me."

"No. But you've been using it," Callie pressed.

"I'm interviewing him," Matilda cut in, damned if she was going to be some silent, pretty handbag for him while the speculation about them raged. "That's it. No romance. No 'might be love.'"

"What are you wearing, Matilda?"

Matilda blinked at the sudden switch in topic. She had a good mind to tell the other woman it was Kmart and normally it wouldn't have been too far wrong, but being a style columnist—for the moment, at least—did give her some perks. She'd rung an upcoming designer she'd recently showcased, who'd been delighted to outfit her.

The dress was a clingy red velvet number that reminded her a lot of *that* dress in *Pretty Woman*. Which seemed appropriate, given that Tanner had paid for the thousand-dollar-a-plate event for her.

But if he expected her to have a condom of every colour in her clutch, he was sorely mistaken.

"It's Simone Cawley."

"And your underwear is from the planet Krypton, I take it?"

Tanner chuckled, and Matilda wanted to scrape her ridiculous stiletto down his calf. She opened her mouth to give a cutting reply, but Callie had already spotted more interesting fish over Matilda's shoulder and was beckoning at a reality TV star. Tanner, still grinning, bowed away graciously, and Matilda was grateful that they were heading indoors, away from the press gaggle and the flashing bulbs.

Once inside, he ushered her to a table and pulled out a chair for her. There was a woman sitting in the seat beside her talking to a man who looked a good ten or fifteen years older than her.

"Tilly, this is Valerie King. Her father is Griffin King, the Smoke's coach."

Matilda had read a fair bit about the enigmatic coach of the Sydney Smoke during her research for the feature series. He was good-looking in a gruff kind of way, and there were a lot of pictures of him scowling. It seemed he didn't suffer fools very gladly.

Matilda smiled at the woman she judged to be a few years younger than her. She was a tall, striking redhead. "Hi, I'm Matilda. Nice to meet you."

Valerie beamed at her, obviously much better at the smiling thing than her father. "Oh, hi. You're the journo writing the features on Slick? I've never laughed so hard than I did over the whole kryptonite panties thing." She grinned, and her eyes twinkled merrily. "I love that the hashtag is still going off on Twitter."

At any other time, Matilda would have been thrilled that something she'd written had gone viral, but given that it had only piqued interest in her and Tanner's relationship, she wished she'd never coined it.

Tanner rolled his eyes and said, "Don't encourage her, Valerie," before introducing Matilda to the guy sitting on Valerie's right. "This is Dan Randall. He sits on the Smoke's executive board."

Dan shook her hand, and the four of them made pleasant conversation as the function centre filled, and other people — who had, according to Valerie, paid a premium to be at Tanner's table — joined them. Matilda was surprised at how easily Tanner schmoozed these days. He hadn't exactly been socially awkward back in high school, but the footy field had definitely been where he was most comfortable.

But here he was in a tuxedo, being witty, entertaining, and generous with his time with the three couples at their table. No question seemed to be off-limits — although, to be fair, most of them were about rugby. He posed for selfies with them and signed paraphernalia they'd brought along, from bumper stickers to footballs to T-shirts. He even danced with each of the women as the jazz band struck up after dinner.

This was exactly the charm that Matilda had written about. But there was nothing forced or disingenuous about it as had been the subtext of her article. This was Tanner just being Tanner, the boy from the country who she'd known since he was fifteen.

"I think it's our turn," he said as he and Valerie arrived back from the dance floor.

Matilda shook her head. "No, thanks." The last thing she wanted was to be held by him, jostled nearer and nearer by the crush of bodies on the dance floor, reminding her of the liberties she'd already allowed him. Tonight had been enjoyable because it *hadn't* been one on one. Because there'd been other people around to dilute his impact.

"You should," Valerie insisted. "He's really very good."

Matilda had no doubt. The man seemed to be good at every damn thing. "Yes, but I, on the other hand, am terrible."

"It's just swaying to music." He smiled, holding his hand out.

"I'll write a thousand dollar cheque to add to the kitty right here, right now, if you dance with him," Dan piped up, pulling a chequebook out of his inner jacket pocket.

Matilda turned startled eyes on the man who hadn't said a lot through most of the night. One thousand bucks? The dress she was wearing seemed more and more appropriate. "What on earth for?"

He shrugged. "Because you two look cute together."

Cute? Matilda blinked. Was the man drunk?

"Go on, Tilly." One of the women sitting opposite winked at her. "Do it for the farmers."

"Yeah," her husband grinned in agreement.

Tanner wiggled his fingers, a smile playing on his full mouth. "Yeah, Tilly. Think of the farmers."

She looked around at all the grinning and expectant faces and Dan with his pen poised. Oh, for the love of…

Matilda sighed and took his hand to the raucous applause of her table. She regretted it instantly as he forged a path through the crowd, too conscious of her hand in his, of the broadness of his shoulders and the exquisite cut of his jacket, of the low buzz spreading like wildfire from one cell to the next until her entire body was humming.

The band was playing "Moon River," the saxophone oozing out its sexy notes as he slid his hand around her back and pulled her in just close enough to allow for the nearby dancers but no closer. His propriety was appreciated, but it was still way too close for Matilda's comfort.

"Happy now?"

He had the good grace not to answer. Or gloat. He just grinned at her as he performed some fancy pivot manoeuvre, pulling her close and spinning them both around a couple of times before easing back from her again.

Matilda's pulse tripped. "Impressive," she murmured. The Tanner Stone she'd known had been a shuffler. "Where'd you learn to dance?"

"Took some lessons a few years back when I was best man for one of the guys. Didn't want to look like a complete heathen."

"The maid of honour was *that* hot, huh?"

He grinned, completely unabashed. "You wound me."

Someone jostled them from behind, forcing them closer, as she had feared. Their proximity ratcheted up the awareness rippling through Matilda's body. In her heels, the top of her head fit neatly under Tanner's chin, and she fought the urge to press her cheek to his shirt. He smelled amazing—no chemical undertone this time—and she wanted to intoxicate herself on the ouzo essence of him as she listened to the slow, steady thump of his heart.

A stark contrast to the rapid trip of hers.

"Thank you for being nicer in your article on Friday." His voice rumbled around her, oozing like notes from the sax.

"No worries."

Matilda had decided to stop giving him such a hard time after the other night. She may have started this thinking of it as killing two birds with one stone—a fast track to features, and revenge on Tanner Stone. But she hadn't found the jerk she'd expected. No matter how mad she was with him over Jessica Duffy.

He'd rebuilt her grandmother's porch railing. And painted it. Then spent an hour in her place hanging art that she'd been neglecting for five years. And the fact that he'd gone down on her and given her a truly spectacular screaming orgasm was as much on her—lying there lapping it up—as on him.

Part of being a responsible journalist was to be impartial. It wasn't a place for revenge, and it shouldn't be coloured by personal baggage.

She was too old to be petty.

So she'd written the article about his early years at the Sydney Smoke with absolutely no agenda. It may not have been effusive but it had been solid and stuck to the facts.

"I was a little disappointed there was no mention of Captain Cunnilingus," he murmured, his mouth near her temple, goose bumps prickling across her scalp.

Matilda glanced around her, her face flushed at the brazen words, hoping no one had overheard. She was hyperaware of where they were, of how many eyes were on them. His large hand rested firmly on the small of her back as if he was he worried she might try to flee such risqué conversation.

He needn't have.

Even if she could push past all the bodies, she doubted

her wobbly legs were up to the task now she was flashing back to the moment his tongue had found, with startling efficiency and precision, *exactly* the right spot. She'd relived it about a hundred times since, and it never failed to quicken her breath or cause a heavy rush of longing between her legs.

But she was annoyed at the amused catch to his voice, and irritated that he was choosing such a public place to flirt with impunity. She guessed this was what he meant by those parting words the other night. *This time, I'm playing to win.*

Matilda straightened her spine as the words circled on an endless loop through her head. No matter how mellow she was becoming, she wasn't in the game anymore, and she'd be damned if she was going to let him turn her on in front of a couple of hundred people. Not without a fight, anyway.

See how he felt taking a little of his own medicine.

"You think," she said quietly, deliberately shuffling her body closer until it was pressed along the length of his, "I should have told everybody that Tanner Stone went down to"—she lowered her voice for dramatic effect—"lady town?"

He chuckled, and it disturbed the wisps of hair at her temple. "Hmm. Maybe that would be a bit too much information."

"Oh, I don't know, Tanner." She tipped her head back to look him in the eye. "A man with a gift like that shouldn't be shy about it."

"I'm gifted, huh?"

Amusement laced his voice, but Matilda could also discern the husky edge to it and was intimately attuned to the tightening of his hand on her back.

Maybe this conversation was having an effect on him, too?

"You should rent a billboard."

If he was confused by her banter, he didn't show it, but he did search her gaze for long moments as they swayed to the music. Long moments during which she became aware of the hardening ridge of his arousal. Her pulse spiked as it pressed with more and more urgency against her stomach.

It *was* having an effect on him.

She shifted against him deliberately, goaded by his brazenness and the wild pulse between her legs. It felt good.

"Any time you want my services, you know my number."

His voice was like gravel now, and it was all she could hear as the world narrowed down to just the two of them, rubbing against each other more than dancing. The music faded, the people pressing in around them faded...*propriety* faded.

"Oh, you do house calls?"

"For you?" His gaze dropped to her mouth before flicking up again. "Absolutely."

"That's very selfless of you."

"Not really. I get *plenty* out of making you come."

Matilda's breath hitched. If that was a line, it was a damn good one. "You wouldn't want a little..." She shifted against him again, and a triumphant buzz coursed through her body as his hand clamped harder in the small of her back. "Something in return?"

He smiled, but it didn't quite reach his eyes. "Only what you're willing to give."

"Like some...necking?"

He stared at her mouth again. "That could be quite nice."

"Maybe"—she slid her hand from his shoulder up into the hair at his nape—"second base?"

His gaze dropped to the artificial depths of her cleavage. "I do like second base."

"What about a...blowjob?"

He glanced up, swallowing hard and huffing out an uneven breath. "I wouldn't say no to that."

"Oh?" she asked innocently. "You like blowjobs?"

"I'm quite partial to them."

"*Really?*" More wide-eyed innocence.

He lowered his lips to her ear. "If you think I haven't been fantasising about your mouth around my cock, then you're crazy."

It was Matilda's turn to swallow, as a mental image of her on her knees sucking his dick, his hand on the back of her head, shimmered like a mirage through her mind.

He was upping the stakes. *Bring it.*

She turned her face, her lips near his ear now. "I remember how you liked me to go deep."

"I liked it any way you gave it."

"Except I didn't swallow."

His half laugh came out all ragged and uneven. "I don't care."

"It's okay," she whispered. "I do now."

"*Christ, Tilly.*" The low groan wound silken fingers around her libido. "You're killing me." His lips brushed the sweet spot behind her ear. "Stop it."

She wasn't exactly doing herself any favours, either, but he'd blinked first and that's all she cared about. As if acknowledging her success, the song came to a close, and couples around them broke apart to clap and cheer.

The bubble around them burst as they followed on automatic pilot, clapping with a great deal less enthusiasm.

"That's all for the dancing for now folks." The emcee's voice boomed around the room. "The band will be back later, but right now its auction time. Let's hear a big round of applause for our celebrity auctioneer, Tanner Stone, captain of the Sydney Smoke rugby team. Where are you, Tanner?"

Tanner blinked, clearly still dazed from the dangerous game of chicken they'd been playing on the dance floor.

"Oh, *Christ,*" he said, turning to her, a fake smile on his face as the crowd on the dance floor parted, the whole room clapping madly as the spotlight hunted him down. "Can you tell I have a raging hard-on?" he whispered.

Matilda dropped her gaze. Well...*she* could tell because she knew, because she'd rubbed herself against the hard, thick press of it. But maybe others wouldn't?

"Better do your jacket up just to be sure," she murmured, the spotlight hitting him as he fumbled with the buttons.

She had to give him points for the grin and wave he gave as the light pooled around him, and for his energetic bounce up to the stage. If he was as sexually bamboozled as she was, he deserved a bloody Oscar.

Matilda made her way back to the table along with everyone else, her head spinning from what had happened out on the floor. She was pleased about the distraction of the auction and the running commentary from Valerie, who seemed to know the ins and outs of the charity and about half the people in the room.

"Does the Smoke call upon Tanner to do this kind of thing very often?"

She supposed, as captain particularly, he had certain commitments that the Smoke lined up for him. Sporting codes were always yammering on about giving back to the community and it was especially loud when one of them found themselves in disgrace.

Valerie frowned. "He's not doing it for the Smoke. This is just one of about a dozen charities Tanner supports in a multitude of ways."

Matilda blinked. "He does?"

"Sure. He comes from a rural community, so Farm Aid is important to him. He also supports several charities who try to reach disaffected youth through sport, then there's the soup kitchen in the Chapel, as well as a couple of literacy ones and a domestic violence shelter. He's probably the most involved with a charity that builds alternative housing for younger people with disabilities requiring care that's traditionally only been available in nursing homes."

Matilda glanced up at the stage as Tanner, his golden-blond hair like a halo under the lights, bantered with the emcee trying to drum up interest in some landscape painted by someone she'd never heard of.

Why hadn't he mentioned any of this? They'd discussed a lot of his life to date, and he hadn't mentioned any of his charity work. She'd just assumed that the soup kitchen he'd taken her to had been a thing he and probably all the other players on his team did every now and then to demonstrate rugby had a social conscience.

There hadn't been anything she'd unearthed online, either. Which didn't mean it wasn't there, but with so much material available about him, inconsequential stuff like charity work probably wasn't a high priority for the run of the mill person who just wanted to look at him with his kit off.

Why look at who the guy *really* was when shirtless *Hey, Girl* memes of him were the first thing that came up in a search engine?

And that included her. She could have dug deeper.

Suddenly Matilda knew the focus for the next feature. Imelda had called him the playboy saint. Little had Matilda known how true that was. She'd been focussing on the playboy bit. Now it was time for the saint.

"Okay, folks, we're down to the last lot in the auction, and you can see from your programmes it's an anonymous item. Now, Tanner, I understand this is from your teammates at the Smoke who wanted to donate for the auction tonight?"

Tanner gave a nervous laugh, and Matilda glanced up from the table where she'd been mentally writing the opening lines of her feature.

"That's right. And all I can say is…apologies in advance," he said. "It was Linc's idea, and we should know by now never to listen to anything Lincoln Quinn has to say."

The crowd laughed and cheered. "But, anyway," Tanner continued, clearing his throat, "the other guys thought it'd be a bit of a hoot, too, and ran with it."

"Well, show us then," the emcee urged. "Put us all out of our misery."

Matilda craned her neck to see what Tanner was holding up. It was something in a frame she couldn't make out from here, and she thanked God for the big screen either side.

People were already laughing and clapping by the time Matilda computed what was it was—two pairs of white, women's underwear. On the front there was something that looked like a glowing green rock of some description and on the back, printed across the booty was KRYPTONITE in block capitals, the lettering done in flaming orange.

Valerie whooped and hollered, laughing as she spontaneously hugged Matilda. "They're perfect." She grinned. "Linc's a genius."

They sold for eight thousand dollars.

Chapter Eleven

The following Friday, Tanner sat in his car outside Tilly's apartment block for an hour before he saw her pull up outside. It should have been a useful heel-cooling period, but he was just as ticked now as he had been when he read her feature article over breakfast.

How fucking could she? He hadn't given her permission to print any of that stuff about his charity work. Hell, he had no idea she was even planning it. He'd foolishly thought after he'd made her come hard and fast, and she'd *almost* returned the favour on a *public* dance floor at a *charity* event, that she was done with pissing him off.

Sure, it had been a bit one step forward, two steps back with her, but he'd sensed things had changed on that dance floor. God…she'd been magnificent, taunting him the way she had. All he'd been able to think about since was her on her knees.

Swallowing.

But apparently, she wasn't done screwing him with yet. She just preferred to do it with her keyboard. And his pants on.

Ever since he'd been press-ganged into this asinine publicity caper by the powers that be, he'd cooperated. Because for some damn fool reason he'd believed the focus would be on football. And yet, so far, he'd had the size of his ego—and his dick—called into question, and suffered through the kryptonite panties debacle.

Not that he'd been particularly bothered by either. Despite what Tilly had written about the big and the *small* of him, Tanner had always been able to laugh at himself, and both had been objectively funny. He'd borne the good-natured ribbing from his teammates and sports journalists with his usual grace and quick-witted smack talk.

Hell, he really only cared what people wrote about him as it pertained to rugby. The rest was like water off a duck's back.

Until today.

He didn't do his charity work for recognition, and he sure as shit didn't want it splashed all over the newspapers.

Christ. Tanner Stone the playboy saint?

She'd actually called him that. The suits had loved it, of course. Social media had gone nuts. The bloody hashtag #playboysaint had been trending on Twitter all frickin' day.

He wasn't any saint.

If she knew how much he'd like to throttle her right about now, or how close he'd come to throwing her over his shoulder and doing her against the nearest wall at the Farm Aid thing the other night, she'd never have called him that.

His first instinct had been to ring her with a piece of his mind. But that was too distant for him—his anger had been too great, demanding a ringside seat as he confronted her. He wanted to see in her face that she understood how pissed off he was.

So he'd taken his ire out on the football field at training, much to the delight of Griff, who was happy to have him back, and the alarm of his teammates, who he'd run ragged and ploughed through at every opportunity.

And now he was here.

He waited ten minutes before he followed her up to her apartment. He might be ticked, but he wasn't going to get into a slanging match with her in the middle of the street. What he had to say was private and personal, and there were too many bloody people with mobile phone cameras for his liking.

He tempered the urge to bash her door down, giving one brief, loud knock, his heart crashing around his chest while he waited for her to open the door.

"Oh, hey," she said with a big welcoming smile that hit him right in the chest. "If it isn't the playboy saint," she teased. "Come in."

Tanner blinked as she slunk away from the door. Her feet were bare, half her leopard-print blouse was untucked from her skirt, she had a glass of wine in one hand, and she'd smiled at him.

Genuinely.

And invited him into her apartment without any kind of caveat. Who was this chick? Had she been drugged? Body snatched?

"Do you want a beer?" she called as she headed in the direction of the kitchen.

Tanner's gaze dropped to the swing of her ass encased in a tight skirt.

Fuck. Why would he even notice that shit when he was so mad at her he could barely think straight? Couldn't she, at least for tonight, be her usual wary and standoffish self instead of warm and welcoming?

"Tanner?" she called.

"No," he said stiffly, pulling the door shut with a bang as he followed her into the kitchen. "I don't want a goddamn beer."

She stopped with her hand on the fridge door and turned with a frown. "Are you okay?"

"No." He glared at her as he halted on his side of the kitchen counter. "I'm not."

"O…kay." She moved to her side of the counter and put her wineglass down. "You look kinda mad."

"Oh, I'm not *kinda* mad," he growled, a hot ball of anger burning in his gut. "I'm blindingly furious."

Her brow furrowed deeper. "At…me?"

"Yes." He shoved his hands on his hips. "At you."

The relaxed line of her body seemed to straighten before his eyes, her gaze growing wary. "You didn't like the article?"

Tanner snorted. "You could say that."

She rubbed her forehead, her face blank, looking genuinely perplexed. "But…I was really nice."

"You were really frickin' out of line, that's what you were."

She blinked. "*What?*"

"I *did not* give you permission to write that stuff about me."

"What do you mean?" She shook her head, clearly confused. "What stuff?"

Tanner's hands dropped to the countertop. "About my charity work."

She was gaping at him now like he'd lost his mind. Tanner kind of felt like he had. How could he be so pissed off and yet so…*distracted* by her all at once?

It did not improve his temper.

"You *didn't* want me to tell the country that the guy who kicks a ball around a field for a stupid amount of money actually spends a shitload of it, as well as his time, on a variety of charities who think you're the second coming?"

"That about sums it up."

Her lips parted slightly as if she wanted to say something but her brain wasn't cooperating. "I…" She shrugged helplessly. "Don't understand."

"That stuff is *private,*" he rasped, through gritted teeth. "*Nothing* to do with anyone else."

"So, you just want them to think you're some…dumb, one-dimensional *jock* who only cares about his rugby and doesn't have any kind of life outside of football?"

"Yes," he hissed, flattening his palms on the benchtop. "That's exactly what I want."

She swiped her wineglass up and took a gulp, eyeing him over the rim, the amber flecks in her opal eyes starting to heat and glow. "Well, *God forbid,*" she snapped, clunking the glass down on the bench, "that someone of your status can also have a social conscience!"

"You don't understand." He shook his head, a pressure building in his chest as he tried to articulate why he was so pissed off. "I don't want any of the charities or the people who work in them or who are a recipient of their work to think I only do this to look good in the goddamn newspaper! Or for some kind of *saintly* social cred. It means more than that. It's not just lip service to me."

"So, why act like it is? What's wrong with exploring that side? I'm doing a six-part feature series about the man behind the image, for crying out loud! What's wrong with saying Tanner Stone isn't just a damn good rugby player? Increasing your charity profile can only be to their benefit, surely? So why are you acting like I just announced on Twitter you like to wear women's underwear? What exactly are you afraid of? Are you ashamed of being anything other than a hard-ass footballer? You think this makes you soft somehow? You think people knowing this stuff will diminish your popularity?"

Tanner snorted, shoving a hand through his hair. She couldn't be serious? "You think I give a *crap* about popularity?" he demanded.

Her eyes bugged. "I think you do when it suits you," she retorted. "I think our friend the maître d would agree that being popular has gotten you a shitload of perks not available to the rest of us mere mortals."

Tanner's face heated as her well-aimed barb found its mark. She was right. It was a bit rich to protest his celebrity when so much of what came to him was *because* of who he was.

And he hated being called on his shit. Especially by Tilly. Especially after that article. But she had him all wrong if she thought he threw his name around willy-nilly.

"God." He shook his head in disbelief. "You seriously don't know me, do you."

"I know you'd rather people think you were just some jock with a pocketful of cash, playing musical women."

"And is that what you think?" he demanded.

"You don't leave me a whole lot of choice."

"Damn it, Tilly," he bit out, thumping his fist down on the benchtop. "You *know* that's not me. Look me in the eye and tell me you know, because if you can't, I'll have to wonder if you ever really knew me at all."

Her indrawn breath was audible as she skewered him with her indignant gaze. Clearly he'd pushed her too far. She was magnificent in her anger. Two high spots of colour stained her cheeks as her gaze narrowed, her chest heaving in and out, her eyes glittering.

How could he be so angry yet so turned on?

"Oh, I know you," she yelled. "You're the kind of guy who not only cheats on his girlfriend but brazenly *flaunts* his infidelity in front of all and sundry, *completely*"—she jabbed the kitchen bench with her index finger—"uncaring about publically tearing my heart out and *humiliating* me in front of everyone we knew." Her face was twisted into a mask of contempt. "I *know* you, Tanner Stone. I know the *real* you."

Tanner's heart pounded hard as her bitter words hit his chest like bullets. He'd thought he'd been making such progress with her, but the events of eight years ago obviously still seethed beneath the surface.

She was still mad.

Well...*so was he*. Today particularly.

Mad that she could be so quick to condemn him, the person she'd *supposedly* loved, without so much as trying to ascertain what had gone down, without *demanding* a single explanation.

He'd been relieved back then that she hadn't, but a part of him had also been disappointed. And hurt—*yes, hurt*—that she'd been so quick to believe the worst of him.

So quick to turn her back.

And right now, angry from the article and her holier than thou attitude and how much, despite all that, he wanted to bend her over the kitchen bench, it still stuck in his craw.

He'd been keeping his temper relatively in check until now but it snapped suddenly with a twang she could no doubt hear. "If you'd *really* known me," he yelled back, "you'd have never believed that *bullshit.*"

She gaped at him, confusion clouding her gaze, but he didn't care. He pushed away from the bench, turning on his heel, and stormed out of her apartment.

• • •

Tanner woke the next morning considerably calmer than when he'd gone to bed. He grimaced at his behaviour. It might have felt good at the time to yell and get it all off his chest, throwing that last cryptic comment at her face, but with some time and space he could admit to being a bit of a dick.

She was right. What did it matter if people knew about his charity work? He may not have wanted it splashed around—

and it *wasn't* because he was ashamed or worried about his popularity or being looked upon as *soft*—but it was hardly the end of the world, either.

He had wanted to keep his involvement in the different charities largely on the down low, largely behind the scenes. The Farm Aid gala had been one of the few exceptions. But maybe she was right. Maybe now he'd been outed, his charities *could* use his name a bit more to their advantage.

Maybe that was the silver lining in this whole frickin' mess he'd caused by storming in and out of her apartment last night with a head full of steam.

Like a total dick.

Christ, but she knew how to push his buttons. Needling him and calling him on his shit. Not backing down or giving him any quarter. Spewing all her still palpable hurt and anger all over him.

Pissing him off and turning him on all at the same time.

Remembering it even now with the benefit of some space, it stirred his pulse *and* his frickin' loins, the confrontation hanging over him like a thunderclap. He didn't need that. He had a game this afternoon, and he couldn't go into it like this. Being angry could sometimes give him an advantage, a focus, but it was more likely to ruin his concentration when he knew that he was to blame for their argument.

And Griff, his team, and the club needed him to be at his best.

He needed to make it right. He certainly needed to apologise.

He swung his legs over the side of the bed and reached for his phone. He scrolled to her number then hesitated. Would she even pick up when she saw it was him? Something in his gut told him she wouldn't so he'd have to try a different approach.

He smiled as he tapped on his Twitter app. At least his

tweeps were on his side. He quickly scrolled through his notifications then opened a fresh tweet, deliberating for a couple of minutes as to the best approach. After starting and discarding several, he settled on something simple.

Forgive me @MatildaK??

Yep. He liked it. It was to the point. And sincere. He sent it out into the ether before he could change his mind, a dozen notifications lighting up his feed almost instantly. Most of them were retweets and of course, rugbybunny1, always quick off the mark, had her say—

Uh oh #playboysaint what did you do to @MatildaK ?? #holysmoke #mightnotbelove???

Curiously, a tweet from Matilda was the next in line. Tanner's pulse kicked up a notch or two. Matilda had never responded to the speculation about them on Twitter, and she'd never responded to him directly.

What did that mean?

It's ok @slickstone. Am over the shock of finding you in my underwear.

Tanner threw his head back and laughed at her goading. He loved it when Tilly was shitty *and* witty all at once. It was those little flashes of the old Tilly that kept him going, that gave him hope that there was a future for them.

Twitter exploded. Tanner literally couldn't keep up with the reaction. And not just from his fans, but from people like Callie Williams and most of the blokey-blokey sports journos he knew. He ignored them all—it was just Tilly he was interested in. He took a few seconds to compose an equally goading reply.

I had to get you out of them somehow
@MatildaK. #mightbelove

He hesitated over using the hashtag and then thought
screw it and hit send. Twitter was going to love it, and if it kept
her a little off balance where he was concerned, then that was
good, too. She thought she had him all figured out? Well…
he'd see about that.

He waited for half an hour for a reply but none was
forthcoming. And clearly none would be. He switched to text.

**Come to the game today. Sit in the box with the WAGS.
Valerie will be there. We can do interview #5 after. You
want to see the *real* me? Come to a game.**

Tanner had no idea if she'd get back to him quickly or not
at all. But from a journalistic standpoint, he couldn't see how
she could resist. Her reply was almost instantaneous.

And brief.

Fine.

He grinned at her passive aggressive response as he
tapped in the reply.

**It's an afternoon game at Henley. Come to the main
entrance at 3. I'll get Val to meet you.**

She didn't bother to reply, but already Tanner was feeling
better. He'd fucked up by making a big deal out of her last
feature article, and things had escalated last night. They'd both
said things that had hurt. But it was probably the conversation
they needed to have. Or at least the opening, anyway.

He had to tell her the truth about what was really behind
that stupid, awful kiss. Maybe she'd stop being so pissed off at
him, and they could move forward. Until now he'd thought

it was better to just leave the past in the past. He hadn't been sure she'd believe him, anyway. But that clearly wasn't working. Maybe it was time to put it all out there?

Bring it all to a head?

Hell, yeah.

He scrolled to Twitter again, ignoring the two-hundred-odd notifications.

If I kick three field goals 2nite I think @MatildaK should grant me a kiss. What say you tweeps? #mightbelove

Tanner tweeted it out to his hundred thousand followers. Three field goals was a big ask, but he arguably had the best damn foot in Australian rugby and was totally up for it.

And he was declaring himself. What was the point of a declaration if it wasn't grand? A thrill of excitement, similar to the one he always felt in those seconds before the starting hooter rang out, tightened his belly.

He'd been waiting for Tilly to come to him.

Not anymore.

• • •

There were about half a dozen women in the Smoke's corporate box, all somehow looking glamorous in jeans and the distinctive blue and silver jerseys of the team. Matilda was also wearing jeans and a cute, silky, button-up shirt but felt somewhat dowdy and out of place in the company of the gorgeous WAGS—wives and girlfriends—of the players. She needn't have. They all made her welcome and even teased her about putting Tanner out of his misery. Apparently not one of them doubted he could kick three field goals if he put his mind to it.

Matilda smiled good-naturedly but underneath it all felt a

little sick about the pledge. On every social media platform she looked #fieldgoalwatch was trending, and everyone, including mainstream media, was talking about her and Tanner.

As if Valerie could sense her nervousness, she took Matilda under her wing, chattering away all bubbly and bright as if it was perfectly normal to be in this world.

It probably was to her. No doubt she'd grown up with it.

They'd sat down next to a woman called Eve who was older than everyone in the room. Maybe forty? She wasn't a WAG, she was Griffin King's personal assistant slash Girl Friday as Valerie had introduced her, and her fifteen-year-old son Liam, who had Down syndrome, was currently down in the locker room with the guys.

He was apparently footy mad—*how could he not be?* Eve had laughed—and the Smoke's unofficial water boy at all their home games. Griff took him out to the sidelines with the rest of the team, and he ran on when any of the players needed a water bottle.

Her eyes shone with unshed tears as she told Matilda how proud she was of him and how grateful she was to her boss for indulging him.

"He's a good man, that father of yours," Eve had said, smiling at Valerie.

Valerie had smiled back, but it had seemed rather strained to Matilda.

About ten minutes before kick off, the big man himself strode into the box. He was quite the presence. Tall and erect, his shoulders still broad, his stomach still flat, still wearing the hell out of a pair of jeans. Good-looking in a grizzly, broken-nosed, silver-fox kind of way.

He didn't bother with preliminaries as his gaze went straight to Eve. "I need you to organise a meeting with the medicos for eleven on Tuesday."

Eve rolled her eyes. "You could have texted me that."

"Needed to stretch my legs," he said gruffly.

"Hey, Dad," Valerie said hesitantly, smiling tentatively at her father.

Matilda blinked at Valerie's transformation from bright and bubbly to timid and uncertain. There was a strange mix of trepidation and hope on the younger woman's face.

Griffin looked almost startled by her presence, pausing before nodding awkwardly. "I didn't know you were coming today." If possible, his voice was even gruffer.

"I come to *every* home game, Dad."

"Oh. Right." He nodded then looked awkwardly around before saying, "Right," again and departing in the blink of an eye.

Matilda glanced at Valerie as silence descended on the room for a moment. A heavy layer of sympathy blanketed the room, and Eve squeezed Valerie's arm.

What the hell was that?

Then one of the women—Matilda thought it was Brett Gable's wife—said, "They're running on," and the atmosphere changed again as all the women, including herself and Valerie, complete with her brittle smile, moved closer to the floor to ceiling glass.

She quickly forgot the Valerie/Griffin thing as she spied Tanner's golden-blond head. Even from this distance, the man looked big, and butterflies wearing jackboots stomped around in her stomach.

Pre-game nerves. Hers. Not his. It took her back.

How many rugby matches had she sat through in those three years she and Tanner had been an item? Too many to count.

Although none of them had been in this kind of luxury.

More like a god-awful hard wooden or freezing metal seat on the first row of the bleachers. But he'd always sought her out as she'd sat on the sidelines, making eye contact before the hooter went. It'd been bad luck if he didn't—one of those odd superstitions sports men were known for.

As if on cue, he looked toward where the box was located, and she swore she could feel his gaze lock on hers.

Certainly the commentary, which was being piped into the corporate box, made note of it, too. Obviously, as the commentators also waited for the hooter, they had nothing better to talk about than Tanner's boast about the three field goals. The commentators laughed, thinking it both hysterical and foolish, and Matilda wanted to die knowing that her and Tanner's *supposed* romance was being discussed on national television.

She'd never been so damn pleased to hear a hooter in her life!

Chapter Twelve

With only five minutes left in the game, the atmosphere in the box was electric. The Smoke were three ahead, and Tanner hadn't yet scored his third field goal. He'd scored the first two in the first half but so far hadn't managed the third.

All the women in the box were plugging for him. The first two Tanner had kicked had elicited exaggerated "Ooooo's" and other such nonsense from the teasing women, and Matilda couldn't help but laugh.

"He's running out of time," Fran Gage murmured, sitting forward in her seat, tearing strips off the label on her beer bottle.

"He'll make it," Valerie assured them, conviction ringing in her voice.

Matilda had a gut feeling Valerie was right. Even at fifteen years old, Tanner's kick had been outstanding. It didn't stop her from feeling physically ill, though, waiting for it.

As if it hadn't been bad enough watching every single bone-crunching tackle and ruck. She'd forgotten how physical the game was. How…gladiatorial.

With two minutes to go, Matilda was sure she was going to throw up. All the commentators were talking about now was Tanner and time running out on his wild field goal bet, and the opposing team had the ball and were running it toward their end.

Then suddenly Tanner, running hell for leather, intercepted the ball, and he was off, looking fresh out of the blocks instead of exhausted from the previous eighty gruelling minutes. The excitement from the crowd and the commentators was electric as everyone in the box leaped to their feet and practically pressed their noses against the glass.

"Oh my God," Fran muttered as Tanner weaved past two opposition players. "He's going to do it!"

A third opposition player lunged for Tanner's legs, getting a hand to his calf, and Tanner stumbled for a second before righting himself and stepping out of the grasp, sprinting away. His eyes never left the goalposts, and within seconds he was right in front of them, not missing a beat as he dropped the ball down to his foot mid-run, kicking it right between the posts.

The Smoke players went wild, all leaping on Tanner's back. The crowd erupted. The commentators went off their nuts. The women in the corporate box all jumped in the air cheering and laughing and dragging Matilda into a big group hug.

"He did it. He did it!" Valerie beamed, her arm slung around Matilda's neck, her brittle smile long gone. "I knew he could do it. You can't turn the man down now."

Matilda looked around at the rest of the group. There seemed to be a consensus, if their faces were anything to go by.

"C'mon. Let's go down and greet the conquering heroes. You," she said, grinning as she grabbed Matilda's hand, "in particular."

Before she could voice any objection or dig in her heels, Matilda was whisked out of the box and ushered down to the field. Her brain was a jumble. She'd tossed and turned most of the night, and been distracted all day, trying to decipher Tanner's last furious words to her.

If you'd really known me, you'd have never believed that bullshit.

And she wasn't any closer to figuring them out. She'd *seen* him sucking Jessica Duffy's face off with her own two eyes. If it had just been something she'd heard, shitty gossip, some kind of whisper that she'd taken as fact then she'd understand his anger.

But she'd *seen* him.

What the fuck else was she supposed to believe? That he was trying to remove a foreign body from her airway?

With his tongue?

And this morning he was back to being his usual charming, flirty, social-media-darling self. Teasing her about a date. Like they'd never argued. Like he'd never called into question how well she'd known him.

Was she supposed to just forget everything—last night *and* that other night eight years ago?

The finish hooter sounded in her ears as she was led past the locker rooms where this whole thing had restarted six weeks ago and was jollied along out through the central tunnel into the night air filled with the noise of a cheering crowd. She was dragged to the sidelines as the two opposing teams shook hands and several commentators with their cameramen ran onto the field, sticking microphones in front of key players.

Matilda watched as the guy called Chuck Nugent tried to get Tanner to talk but was resoundingly ignored and none too happy about it, either. Tanner didn't seem to care, searching the sidelines with his hungry blue eyes.

Matilda knew the exact moment he found her, his gaze fixing firmly on her, pinning her to the spot.

"Oh, Lordy," Fran whispered to her as Tanner headed in her direction. "That man is going to kiss you hard."

Matilda swallowed. Her mouth was dry. Her breath stuck in her throat. Her heart pounded like a drum in her chest. It was like that night on the dance floor as everything faded to black around them. No excited WAGS, no chanting crowd, no news cameras. Just Tanner striding across the grass with purpose in his step and her in his sights.

Suddenly hands were at her back, propelling her forward, and she was walking toward him as if on autopilot. She could see the wet cling of his jersey to his pecs, the sweat plastering his fringe against his forehead and the ripple of thorns across his biceps as he drew closer.

He loomed big and powerful and had eyes only for her.

Just like the smooth motion of that drop kick, he didn't break stride when he finally reached her, sliding a hand onto her waist and jerking her against him. She only had a second to register the puffiness of his right eye where he'd copped an elbow, before his lips came down on hers in a crushing kiss that unleashed a mushroom cloud of lust through her system, demanding her absolute surrender.

Which she gave with absolutely no resistance, moaning against his mouth as she clung to his broad shoulders.

She was vaguely aware of the crowd going crazy. Of the chant, "*Kiss her, kiss her, kiss her,*" echoing around the field. Of clicks and flashes and lights from TV cameras.

But nothing mattered more than the hungry dominance of Tanner's mouth, the hard wall of his chest, and the earthy, sweaty smell of him filling up her head, making her crazy.

"So, can he kiss as well as he kicks?" Chuck Nugent asked, a fluffy microphone thrust in their direction, interrupting their union.

Tanner's mouth broke from hers as abruptly as it had joined. Matilda was pleased he was still holding her tight, as her legs nearly buckled.

"We're all hanging out at my place later," he said, his voice low, almost a growl, ignoring Chuck and the furor around them, eyes only for her. "Join us."

It wasn't a request. Somewhere in her muddled brain, Matilda recognised she should say no. She should pull away. She should demand an explanation about what he'd said last night. But she didn't have the brainpower—no, *will*power—to deny him.

She simply nodded and said, "Okay."

• • •

Everything was a bit of a haze after that. Chuck creepily followed her off the field, and Matilda was grateful for the protection of the WAGS who ushered her away to the corporate box to wait out the post-game formalities. They all watched probably rugby's most entertaining press conference ever on the television screen in the box as Tanner faced more questions about those three field goals and the kiss then the actual game itself.

The officials tried to keep steering it back on track, but the media seemed to be interested in only one story and Tanner bantered with them easily while giving nothing away.

Eventually, some kind of official came along to the box and escorted them all out of the front door of the clubhouse where a chauffeured minibus with a handful of Smoke players, all showered and changed and talking smack, were waiting.

All the women filed in, grabbing seats next to their partners. Valerie disappeared down the aisle, too, which just left Matilda standing there. Tanner patted the seat beside him, smiled at her, and said, "Come sit here."

Matilda slid in, her heart tripping at how well he wore casual—jeans encasing powerful quads, a grey-blue T-shirt taut across his pecs, his hair darker now it was damp. There were no signs of fatigue. Or injury for that matter, save for just some slight puffiness around his eye now. But he must hurt. She'd lost count of the number of times he'd been stomped on in tackles.

"Hey, here's our lucky charm," Linc called out from the back.

"Yeah, Tilly," Dex said from behind. "Keep the man hanging and challenge him to four field goals next week."

Everyone laughed, and Tanner performed quick intros as the van started to move. In an effort to ignore how the sway of the van caused their arms and legs to brush together, Matilda tuned into the banter and laughter being thrown around the van with comfort and ease.

Tanner copped the most, but he gave as good as he got. It was obvious they were all close, like a family more than a team.

"You're quiet," he murmured in her ear, his breath warm on her neck. "You okay?"

The low timbre of his voice trailed light fingers across her belly, the muscles beneath reacting as if the caress had been real. "Yes."

He didn't press her, and Matilda was relieved to be at his place thirty minutes later and able to escape his close proximity. Her resistance to him was crumbling at a rate of knots.

How could she be so conflicted over him yet want him so badly? Was it just muscle memory?

Or more?

It was eight o'clock by the time everyone was walking into Tanner's gorgeous apartment in Finger Wharf. She knew he lived here. She knew they were expensive and exclusive—

hell, *movie stars* owned apartments here—but she wasn't prepared for its magnificence. Not that the inside was any kind of *Home Beautiful* show pony. It was definitely a man's pad, but the location, with the wharf extending right out into the harbour, was something else.

It sure as shit put her Potts Point apartment to shame.

Clearly, everyone else had already been here as she was the only one walking around with her mouth open.

"I'll show you round later," he murmured, all low again, his hand on her hip just as Valerie bounced over and said, "You have to come check out his awesome view," and Linc said, "Where are those damn pizzas you bribed us with?"

The view was indeed awesome, with Sydney's skyline laid out before her, dramatically punctuated by Centrepoint tower rising into the night sky. Closer to the apartment, the lights from the restaurants that ran the length of the wharf reflected in the surface of the harbour. She could hear a low murmur of voices floating up from below and hear the occasional slap of water against wood.

It had always been a fantasy of Matilda's to live somewhere with a sea view. This wasn't exactly the beach but hell…it was the next best thing.

The pizza arrived fifteen minutes later and they all sat around, some on chairs, some on the floor, and ate. Matilda had deliberately chosen to sit on the couch between two of the WAGS—she wasn't sure she could cope with Tanner being too near again.

He sat in an armchair a few feet away, the smile on his face telling her he knew exactly what she was up to.

The casual meal was fun. There were five couples—*not* including her and Tanner because they *weren't* a couple—plus four single guys—Linc, Dex, Bodie, and Ryder—and Valerie. They sat around talking and laughing about a variety of subjects, not just the game. They seemed to enjoy each other's company even if that meant taking turns at being the brunt of merciless razzing.

One thing was clear, she had plenty of fodder for her next feature and an angle—how much he was loved and respected. Because it was clear here tonight that everyone *loved* Tanner. Sure, there was trash talk, but she could see right through it to the respect and affection that underpinned it. And it wasn't just because he was their captain, either. It was because of his generosity of spirit. He'd praised all the guys for their part in the win today, and every one of them had sat a little taller in their seats.

It shouldn't come as any surprise. Tanner had always been well liked because, quite simply, he'd always been one of the nicest guys around. Apart from the *incident* with Jessica Duffy, he'd never put a foot wrong.

His mother had brought him up to be kind, respectful, and decent, and students, teachers, his fellow players, coaches, and even his opponents had liked him. He'd been polite, well-manner and always ready to lend a hand if someone needed it.

What *wasn't* to love?

Matilda dragged her thoughts away from that dangerous question, switching her attention to Valerie teasing Linc about being a glutton as he wolfed down the last slice of his *second* pizza. If she wasn't very much mistaken, it may have even bordered on flirting. Linc razzed her back about his manly appetite in a very *brotherly* fashion.

Hmm. *Interesting.* She leaned toward John Trimble's wife, Kathy, who sat beside her. "Is Linc blind?" she whispered. "Valerie's gorgeous and flirting?"

Kathy smiled and whispered back, "No messing with the coach's daughter."

"That's an order from the coach?" Griffin King had barely acknowledged his daughter. Why would he care?

Kathy shook her head. "Not in so many words. It's kind of an unspoken law. But Griff is too much of an enigma for anyone to push that envelope even a little."

Matilda glanced at Valerie. Poor girl. Growing up around all this beefcake and not able to nibble at some of the hamburgers.

After the pizza had been eaten and the boxes thrown out, a more in depth dissection of the game started and Matilda wandered out with her glass of wine to the deck to admire the view again. Watching the New Year's Eve fireworks from here must be breathtaking.

"Not too shabby, huh?"

She turned to find Kathy joining her. John Trimble was the oldest member of the team and his wife was about thirty. "I think I could hack it," Matilda smiled.

"Play your cards right and that might be a possibility," she teased. "I don't think I've ever seen our Tanner quite this smitten."

Well. *That was direct…*

Matilda took a sip of her wine to cover the sudden knot of nerves tightening her throat. "It's complicated," she said lamely.

Kathy eyed her shrewdly. "Is it?

Matilda tried to smile again as the first tendrils of irritation crawled up her spine. "Look, I know all the guys think the sun shines out of his—"

Her laugh interrupted Matilda. "It's not just the guys. If it wasn't for Tanner, John wouldn't still be playing rugby. He was almost cut from the team after he injured his ACL three years ago. He was in his mid-thirties and had a bunch of niggling injuries. It was Tanner's first year as captain, and he went to bat for him."

Kathy paused and sipped her wine, her hand gripping the railing as she stared into the lights on the harbour surface.

"Tanner insisted that they needed guys like John with his level of experience on the team, and then he trained with John every day in secret sessions to make sure his knee was indestructibly strong after the operation. John's playing better rugby than he's played in his life. He's been picked for the Australian team the last two years. As far as *I'm* concerned, the sun *absolutely* shines out of Tanner Stone's ass. "

Matilda would have been able to hear the passion and conviction in Kathy's voice from the other side of the harbour.

"Men like that don't come along often," she said, dropping her hands from the railing.

With a squeeze of the arm and a quick, easy smile, Kathy departed. Matilda watched her before turning back to gaze at the skyline. She had to admit Kathy was right. Men like Tanner were rare. She'd always known that deep down. She'd known it eight years ago, and everything she'd seen of him in the last six weeks had confirmed it.

Helping with her grandmother's porch, hanging paintings, his charity work, the story about John…

So why had he cheated? He'd always had such a strong moral code and belief system. She'd have never thought it of him, and even now, she couldn't believe it was something he would have done casually. So…why?

Had she driven him to it?

Maybe she had? Maybe *she'd driven him to it*. Because Matilda couldn't see why a guy who just didn't *do* that kind of thing had gone and done that kind of thing.

Maybe she'd held out on him too long? They'd gone out for three years, but she hadn't wanted to rush into sex, had wanted to be sure. About him and herself. She'd only decided to take that last step six months before they broke up. She'd thought he'd been okay with that, but maybe deep down he hadn't been?

It had sure as hell seemed like everyone on his team was

doing it toward the end there.

*Oh, God…*what if she hadn't been that good and he hadn't had the nerve to tell her? Or maybe it was because she hadn't let him go down on her?

She'd bet Jessica freaking Duffy hadn't been so bloody fussy.

Ultimately, it didn't really matter. There was no excuse for his cheating. But maybe she needed to look at her part in it. What had she done or not done to drive him to another woman's arms?

It might not have been the sex thing. It could have been other things. Maybe it was time to ask. To have that conversation. To tackle the elephant in the room.

And the even bigger conundrum? If it *was* her fault in some way, no matter how small, but he was here now and he plainly wanted to try again, maybe she should give that a shot?

Maybe with maturity, wisdom, and *experience,* they could be really great together.

Matilda was in the kitchen washing up the wineglasses when she heard the door to Tanner's apartment close. It was almost midnight, but she wasn't tired. Tanner had been staring at her all night, a look of strained anticipation warming his gaze, and she was *alive* inside.

"I thought they'd never go," he murmured as he prowled toward her, stopping about an arm's length away, parking his butt against the edge of the bench.

Matilda's heart thudded in her chest as he crossed his arms and the thorns decorating his biceps bulged in her peripheral visions.

He nodded to the sink. "You don't have to do that."

Oh, yes, she did. If she didn't do something with her hands, she just might put them all over him. Those biceps would be a good place to start. Or maybe down the front of his jeans.

"You got a guy for this, too?"

His mouth kicked up at the side. "You want another drink?" He pushed away from the bench and headed for the fridge, which was behind her.

"I…should go."

He didn't seem too perturbed by her announcement. Its complete lack of conviction probably had something to do with it.

She heard him rustling through the fridge as she stared at the bubbles in the sink. There was the *tink* of glass against marble and then the sound of a cupboard opening. She could hear liquid pouring next, then a soft twisting noise of a lid being opened.

She could sense him drawing nearer again, her nipples tightening, the hairs at the back of her neck standing to attention as heat enveloped her from behind. He stepped in close, the front of his body almost touching the back of hers.

A glass, half filled with pale yellow wine, was placed on the bench near her hip. His beer bottle was slid into place on the other side. He nuzzled his nose along the line of her nape, and Matilda felt it deep inside her belly.

"You want the grand tour?"

She shut her eyes as the serration of his warm breath created havoc in places just *south* of her belly. She wanted to snake her arm up around his neck, to arch her back and purr, rubbing herself against him. She wanted him to slide his hands onto her hips then up to her breasts and pinch her aching nipples hard between his fingers.

God help her, she shouldn't. But she did.

She shook her head.

"No?" he whispered, his hands finding her hips as his body

fully aligned with hers, the bulk and the heat of him trapping her against the sink. "What *do* you want?" he murmured, the flat of his tongue swiping up the side of her neck now.

Matilda grabbed hold of the edge of the sink as her knees gave a precarious wobble. She should be asking him about his cryptic comments, about what *had* gone down that night eight years ago if it really *hadn't* been what she'd seen with her own two eyes. But if she asked him now, before what was *surely* imminent sex, and it started a fight, they might never get around to the sex bit.

And, God help her, she wanted to feel Tanner Stone deep inside her so bad right now she was fully prepared to fuck first and ask questions later.

Fully prepared to hate herself in the aftermath.

She just *had* to have him. Even if it was only once.

"Tilly," he groaned, grinding against her, one hand gliding up just as she'd wanted, cupping a breast, his thumb sliding in delicious torment over the proud, taut peak of her nipple. The other headed down into her jeans, pushing past the waistband of both denim and the lace beneath, zeroing in on more taut, aching flesh, standing just as proud, begging to be touched.

Matilda gasped and bit her lip. "*Taaaanner*," she moaned, her pulse roaring in her head as she turned in his arms.

Chapter Thirteen

Her mouth devoured his. Or maybe his devoured hers. Matilda wasn't keeping score. She just hung on to those big shoulders, opened her mouth, and gave him everything she had, demanding the same in return.

She greedily ate the groan that seemed to come from the pit of his stomach and gave him one back, pressing herself harder against him, standing on her tiptoes, needing to feel the hardness that was rubbing against her belly rubbing against the spot between her legs, where his fingers had been only seconds ago.

She moaned in frustration as she tried to facilitate it, half climbing his big frame to hit the jackpot. Without breaking his liplock, Tanner hauled her up, grinding against the middle seam of her jeans, giving her exactly what she craved. She gasped, breaking the kiss as a million stars burst behind her eyes, her entire body shuddering in pre-emptive satisfaction.

He looked at her, his blue eyes blazing heat and intensity even though his eyelids were at half-mast. "You want me there?" he demanded, his voice low and throaty as he rubbed himself obligingly in just the right spot.

Matilda gasped again, her arms anchoring hard around his neck as she tilted her pelvis to maximise the effect. "Yes, *God yes*, don't stop."

"Hold on," he said, sliding his hands under her thighs, fitting her more snugly against the large bulge in his jeans as he pulled away from the kitchen bench.

Matilda wasn't sure where he was taking them—she assumed the bedroom—she just held on like he asked, kissing him like he was oxygen and she was drowning, riding the hard edge of his cock for all she was worth. By the time he dumped her on the bed, she was about as close to an orgasm as was possible, fully clothed.

She grunted as Tanner's weight came down on hers, but she didn't pause to collect her breath. She clawed at his clothes, dragging his T-shirt up and off his head, sliding her hands all over his magnificent chest.

A red graze marred the skin covering his ribs, almost from nipple to belly button, a tag from where an opponent's boot had left its mark. She traced it with her finger, remembering that he'd just played a bruisingly rough game of elite rugby.

"Are you sore?

He shook his head. "No more than usual."

"You want me to be gentler?" she teased.

"Hell no."

Just what she wanted to hear as she lowered her hand to his fly, fumbling it down, reaching inside and freeing the hard jut of his cock.

"*Fuck*," he groaned, burying his face in her shoulder as she squeezed it.

"Jesus," she murmured, her fingers clamping around his girth, palming it, refamiliarising herself with every contour. "I'd forgotten how well hung you were."

He let out a shaky laugh, lifting away slightly to look

down at her. "I'd forgotten how you could almost make me come just from touching it."

Breathlessly, she stroked him from root to tip as their gazes locked. "I think, from memory, I actually *did* that the first time."

He laughed again, all low and sexy. "You did."

"Do you remember this?" she asked, pushing against his chest, eager to get fully reacquainted.

He didn't budge.

"Move," she muttered.

"Why?"

But the look on his face told her he knew exactly why she wanted him to move. "I want to see if I remember what you taste like," she said, leaning up to run her tongue down the prickly sweep of his throat.

Liquorice allsorts. Is that what he'd taste like down there?

"No way." The deep rumble of his voice tickled her lips as her tongue lapped at the thick slow bound of his carotid pulse.

"I used to love the taste of you." And she had. She'd also loved the power having him in her mouth gave her, knowing he'd have begged her for it if she'd demanded it.

She pushed against him again, hoping to catch him off balance. But he wasn't about to give her any advantage, caging her firmly against the mattress.

"I'm not going to disgrace myself in front of you again."

"Oh?" she teased, slowly gliding her hand up and down the length of him now. "Where's all that tough guy rugby stamina?"

It was satisfying to feel the involuntary thrust of his hips. "I've had a hard-on for you for the last six weeks." His teeth were gritted, his voice a husky growl. "I went home that night after I went down on you and jacked off in the shower. Hell, I don't think I've jacked off this much since I was thirteen. I'm barely hanging on, Tilly, and your mouth isn't going *anywhere* near my cock until we've taken the edge off."

He reached down, yanking her hands away, trapping them both above her head with one big hand as his mouth descended.

Matilda gasped as he zeroed in on her nipple through the fabric of her shirt, her eyes rolling back in her head as he sucked it hard, his teeth scraping, almost bruising in their treatment.

It felt so damn good.

"More," she moaned, arching her back.

He gave her more, still holding her one-handed, his other making short work of her shirt and bra, releasing her hands to get her out of them before throwing them on the floor. He gazed at her small breasts like they were a gourmet delight, and she felt the way she always had when he looked at them like that—like she had a glorious set of double Ds.

He lowered his head, and his mouth was merciless against the bare peaks of her nipples, teasing them with teeth and tongue, grazing and sucking until the heat between her legs roared like a furnace, the sweet torture almost too much to bear.

All she could do was cling to the smooth heat of his shoulders as she mindlessly begged him to put her out of her misery.

"You want this?" he asked, shoving her jeans and pants off her hips.

"Yes," she gasped, lifting her hips, helping him, wanting them off and gone and his dick, so tantalisingly out of reach, buried to the hilt.

"This?" His fingers slid from her clit and burrowed inside her.

A dry sob broke from her throat. "Please...Tanner... please."

"What?" he panted, his eyes glittering down at her as he

watched her face contort with each thrust of his fingers, like he was a puppet master pulling strings in some very intimate places.

"I need you inside me," she gasped, arching her back as he plunged his fingers in nice and hard.

"I am inside you," he grinned, crooking his fingers, hitting a spot that just about made her lose her mind.

Matilda shook her head, pulling at his shoulders. "All of you. I need all of you."

Even three-quarters of the way to insanity, the truth in her words hit hard. She didn't just mean the steady shove of his fingers or the hard thrust of his cock, but everything he had to give. She'd had it once, and, God help her, she wanted it again.

She needed all of him.

He kissed her and tears burned hot behind her closed lids. He slid his fingers out and Matilda whimpered, grabbing his arm, trying to stop him.

"Hang on, baby," he said, pulling away to reach into his back pocket.

Tanner stood, his erection standing proud from the opening of his zipper as he grabbed a foil packet from his wallet. Hastily, he discarded his half undone jeans and underwear and, reaching down, he yanked Matilda's off, too.

All she could do was watch, her chest tight at the sheer masculine beauty of him. Tanner had always been magnificent—something that could only be truly appreciated in his naked form. But he wasn't a teenager any more. He was a man, and he had a *man's* body, with all the subtle differences wrought by maturity.

The sight of him stole her breath and filled her heart with an overwhelming sense of rightness. Of belonging.

Him to her. And her to him.

He quickly rolled the condom on then crawled onto the

bed, settling over her but holding the weight of his torso above her slightly, balancing on the flats of his forearms.

"You were always the best part of me," he said, his voice tremulous as his eyes roamed over her face and his fingers brushed the lobes of her ears. "Always."

Tears pressed behind her lids again as he kissed her hard and long and slow—like he used to. She clung to him, kissing him back as he slid the thickness of his cock through the slickness between her legs, setting up a torturously slow rhythm.

"Tanner," she gasped, breaking off as muscles deep inside her started to spark and pulse. "*Please, I…*"

"Shh," he murmured, kissing her again, his fingers ploughing into her hair, his thumbs at her jaw, tilting it to gain deeper access to her mouth.

The thick, blunt prod of him, notching himself at her entrance, shot the sparks higher, forking up her spine like a streak of lightning. Her hands convulsively gripped his biceps as she shamelessly wrapped her legs around him, easing his first deep, gratifying thrust. She gasped, the kiss broken, at the welcome invasion, everything tight and hot and full, stretching and pulsing and exploding behind her eyes and deep inside her pelvis.

Matilda anchored the backs of her calves to the backs of his thighs, holding him there tight—*right there*—buried to the hilt, and everything seemed to stop as if they were held together in a moment of suspended animation, pulsing together as one.

"Tilly," he groaned in her ear on a roughly exhaled breath. His mouth was pressed to her neck and even just that sensation was too much for a nervous system at flash point. "I have to move. I…need to…"

Tilly loosened her grip on his buttocks. *She needed it, too.*

The rhythm of his hips took over, rocking her high and

hard with each stroke, the walls of her world collapsing in all around her so quickly.

Too quickly.

Everything dissolved as he reared over her, and she clung to his biceps, feeling the flex and bunch of them. Everything quivering and clenching. Everything rippling and spiralling. Until they were both lost in a storm of pleasure, calling out each other's names, one pounding, the other clinging, both working in tandem, stroke for stroke, until neither of them had anything else to give, and they collapsed in a heap on the bed.

They dozed for a while. Tanner didn't know for how long. All he knew was he woke a little later, her ass pushed against a cock that was telling him it wasn't done yet.

He kissed her neck and stroked a nipple, rousing her slowly until she turned in his arms, not talking, not asking, just exploring each other's bodies, this time with a languorous thoroughness that kindled his hopes of a burgeoning connection between the two of them.

Something more than physical. Something deeper.

He lay in a glorious post-coital haze in the aftermath, malaise invading his bones, the still darkness of the night blanketing them in a drowsy cocoon. Tilly was smooshed up along his side, her head on his chest.

Having her here tonight in his apartment, with the guys and their wives, having a good time, all relaxed and laughing, had seized great big handfuls of his gut and squeezed. This was his world. Rugby. His teammates. Tanner had hoped she'd fit in. He'd *hoped* that she'd like his friends, that she'd embrace his world, too.

And she certainly seemed to.

His fingers trailed from the curve of her shoulder to the dip of her waist then back again. Her fingers drew patterns on his chest before wandering to his biceps to trace the outline of his tattoos.

"Why thorns?" she asked after a while.

Tanner, whose eyes had been drifting shut, stirred himself, resuming his stroking, goose bumps roughening the pads of his fingers in their wake. "I liked the symbolism," he murmured. "You want to get past me then you're going to have to hack me down."

"Tough guy, huh?"

He swore he felt her lips curve against his chest. "When it comes to rugby? Sure."

When it came to her? To love? He was weak as piss.

But not anymore. It was past time he put things right with her.

"I'm sorry," he said tentatively, aware that his heart was suddenly thudding loudly in his chest as his palm came to rest on the spread of her ribs, "about how…things ended between us."

The stroke of her finger halted abruptly, and she grew very still.

"If I could do that moment over again, I would."

He would have been honest. He would have used his words instead of a dumb, ill-considered, *rash* action. *Made* her see the sense in not following him. In pursing her own dreams.

Her cheek tensed against his pec, and he swore her lungs hadn't inflated since he'd opened his mouth. "It's fine," she said, her voice toneless. "I've pretty much come to the conclusion that it must have been something I'd done anyway."

It was Tanner's turn to still *and* to tense. *What the fuck?* What the hell was she going on about? He frowned down at her blonde head. "What?"

She shrugged, her fingers resuming their patterns on his

arm. "I've been angry at you and blaming you all this time, but I realised today that everyone loves you, and that's because you really *are* a great guy." Her voice sounded surprisingly calm and matter-of-fact. "You always were. And you've proven that to me over and over these last six weeks. So it has to have been me. I mean, it does take two people to ruin a relationship, right? Maybe there was something I did or didn't do that drove you to Jessica Duffy? I mean, I made you wait a really long time for sex. And I wouldn't…swallow or let you go down on me. Maybe if I'd been more open to…things you wouldn't have found the need to go elsewhere."

Tanner hadn't known what to expect when he'd opened his mouth to confess all. It certainly hadn't been a *mea culpa* from Tilly.

She was blaming herself now? Because she hadn't been comfortable with certain sexual things?

He hadn't heard anything so crazy in his life.

"That," he muttered, curling himself up into a sitting position, displacing Tilly in the process, "is utter *bullshit*."

He glanced over his shoulder at her, the sheet twisted between her legs covered nothing much at all. Her breasts were bare, as were most of her legs. Just a swath of skin from hip to thigh was hidden from his view. His dick twitched. Even in her state of obvious confusion, frowning up at him, he wanted to rip that sheet away and bury his face in the bit he couldn't see.

He hauled himself out of bed, away from the temptation of her. It was important she hear the *real* reason—that she *understand* his real reasons.

This was not the time for distraction.

"*Nothing* that happened that night was because of anything you'd done or not done. I didn't kiss Jessica Duffy because I was dissatisfied with our sex life and looking for something else. I kissed her on purpose. I waited until you walked through that door and I knew you were looking at me, and I kissed her because I wanted to smash a gulf *so* wide between us that you'd never want to speak to me ever again."

She didn't look any less confused as she swung her legs over the side of the bed, dragging the sheet around her. But she did look pissed off. "Well, congratulations, it worked," she said, her voice stony. "You know, if you didn't want me anymore, you could just have said."

"Didn't want you?" The accusation felt like a hot poker being thrust into his gut. Tanner shook his head. "I never stopped wanting you. Hell, I was all set to ask you *to marry* me. I'd even put a deposit on a ring. I was going to propose and suggest we set a date for after you got back from America."

He shoved a hand through his hair, remembering how excited he'd been to find the perfect ring. A round opal surrounded by diamonds. The stone had been stunningly beautiful and reminded him of her blue-green eyes, complete with a rich fiery vein of pink and amber.

"But then you announced you weren't going to go, were going to knock back your scholarship and do your degree externally in Australia whilst following me around, and all my pleas that you go, that you *not* stay, fell on deaf ears."

She rose from the mattress, pulling the sheet out of the end, wrapping herself up in it as she turned to face him. "So you *kissed* another woman?" she demanded, the rush of air in and out of her chest audible. "To make me *jealous*? To make me…hate you?"

He swallowed. "Yes."

"Jessica *freaking* Duffy?"

Tanner wasn't very proud that he'd chosen Tilly's nemesis deliberately. But it'd had the desired effect. "Yes. I figured she'd cut the deepest. But don't blame her—it wasn't her fault. She had no idea what I'd planned, either."

"Oh, *trust* me," Tilly fumed. "I don't. You are *totally* on the hook for that one." She glared at him across the bed. "How far did it go?" she demanded. "Did you *fuck* her?"

"*No!*"

"Really? Because you both appeared to be enjoying it to me."

Tanner shook his head vehemently. "As soon as you ran out, I broke it off. It was only *ever* a kiss. And a pretty terrible one at that." He shuddered thinking about it now. "Too wet. Too much tongue. It felt like she was trying to reach my balls via my throat."

"Imagine how *not* sorry I am," she hissed, "to hear it was so *freaking* unpleasant for you."

Tanner shoved a hand through his hair, trying to figure out how they'd gone from so deep inside each other he hadn't been able to tell where he ended and she started, to glaring at each other across a mattress that may as well have been as wide as the bloody ocean.

What he'd done had been stupid, but his motives had been true. Surely she could see why he'd done it?

"I'm sorry," he apologised again. "But I did it for you."

Her eyes practically bulged out of her head. "How very noble of you," she yelled, looking around the floor before bending over to scoop up her discarded underwear. "You want a *medal* for your sacrifice?" she demanded as she stepped into the scrap of satin and lace he'd yanked off her less than two hours ago, manoeuvring them up under the sheet.

"Okay, that came out all wrong," he muttered. *Christ.* Talk about making it worse.

"Ya think?"

She threw her shirt on over her head sans bra, yanking the sheet down and off. He quickly located his underwear and pulled them on. Being the only buck naked one in an argument did not augment his position.

"I just meant it was the only way I could think of to make

you dump me and go follow your dreams."

"You think you did me such a *big* favour?" Her voice broke a little, and the sharp edge of it stabbed straight into the middle of his chest. "By *breaking my heart?* And making me distrust not only *every single man* who's crossed my path since, but *myself?* Distrust my own judgement? Making me wary of relationships and getting too close to anyone in case they crushed my heart like *you* did? Closing me off to any possibility of loving another man, or letting him love me?"

Christ. Tanner hadn't wanted that. He'd let her go so she could have a life. *Her* life. "Tilly—"

"*Goddamn it*, Tanner," she yelled, interrupting him with all the grunt of a machete. "My name is Matilda!"

She grabbed her jeans that were in a pile on the floor at the bottom of the bed and turned on her heel, striding for the door.

Chapter Fourteen

"Wait," Tanner called after her, using the superior length of his stride to catch her as she reached the door, grabbing her by the elbow. She flapped her arm trying to yank out of his reach, but Tanner was going to hold tight this time instead of letting her go.

It had been a mistake doing that eight years ago, the gravity of which was only hitting him now.

"Please...*Matilda*, just wait." He dodged another elbow, although he doubted it would have had the same impact as the one he'd copped on the field earlier in the night. He bundled her up in his arms, pressing her back against the wall near the door, shoving a thigh between her legs as she tried to kick at him, caging her with his body.

"I'm sorry, okay? I'm really sorry," he murmured. "I didn't mean for any of that to happen. I was a complete dumbass."

"You got that right," she panted, still pushing against his body.

He was excruciatingly aware of where his thigh was trapped and how every wriggle rubbed her crotch against it. Of the smell of sex still clinging to their skin and sizzling off them like steam as the heat between them grew. Of the frantic pull of her breath and the mad flutter of the pulse in the hollow at the base of her throat.

And, God help him, he was so damned turned on he could barely think for the blood pounding through his head and his chest and his groin. It was the most inappropriate time to get a hard-on.

But his dick didn't get the memo.

She twisted her hips to dislodge him, to no avail, her gaze burning. "Let. Me. Go."

Tanner held fast. "We have the chance to start again, Matilda. You're crazy if you think this thing between us is dead. The chemistry between us is as hot as it always was."

"Speak for yourself," she snapped.

Her denial pushed Tanner to his limit. *No.* No more lies. His lie in their past had already caused too much pain, and he was determined another one wasn't going to derail their future. He wasn't going to let her lie to him *or herself* about what was going on between them.

He pressed his thigh hard between her legs, grinding for good measure, the action hitching her up the wall a little. His erection, straining against the confines of his underwear, pressed into her belly.

He was gratified to hear her sharp intake of breath. "You were saying?"

"That's physics." She dismissed the evidence through gritted teeth. "Not chemistry."

"Bullshit."

He ground again, and she moaned, clutching his biceps reflexively. Her head fell back against the wall, a hot sizzle of lust burning in her gaze. "You better be prepared to follow through on that," she growled, her chest heaving, her voice thick with barely suppressed desire.

Tanner blinked at her very clear meaning.

She wanted to fuck?

Now? Part of him recoiled from the suggestion. They needed to talk. They needed less *action* and more *conversation*. But the blatant intent in her gaze had grabbed him by the dick, and the devil had him by the balls.

"On this?" He ground his thigh into her underwear again.

Holding his gaze she bucked her hips and rode the hard wedge of it. "Yes," she gasped, her hands suddenly in his hair, pulling his head down, their lips meeting in a clash that threw sparks and almost cut Tanner off at the knees.

Their breathing was loud between them as he fought her for dominance of the kiss. Rage at himself for his weakness and frustration at her manipulation combined in a potent mix. The kiss was his to master and damned if he was going to let her have it all her own way. He demanded her submission, and he wasn't letting up until he had it.

But she gave him no measure, twisting and evading any attempt of his to master it, the savage kiss stoking his arousal to fever pitch. And hers, if the whimpery noises coming from the back of her throat were any indicator.

Her submission was brief but splendid, her body softening and melting, a sigh on her lips for the merest of moments. Triumph surged through his system for a nanosecond before her hands were delving inside his underwear, squeezing his cock and cupping his balls, owning him more completely than any kiss could.

"Fuck me," she demanded against his neck, her teeth nipping as she twined her legs around his waist, the fingernails of one hand sinking into the broad sweep of his shoulder, the other guiding his cock to her centre, using the head to push her underwear aside. He settled amidst the slick heat between her legs and Tanner's eyes clamped shut as the sensation pushed him beyond all reason.

This was all kinds of fucked up. They were angry. This wasn't the slow, tender lovemaking of less than half an hour ago—this was *screwing*. One hundred percent pissed-off, nail-raking, neck-biting, wall-fucking *screwing*.

It was rage and revenge. It was reprisal. It was rutting like animals.

It sure as hell *wasn't* the way to prove to her that he wanted more from her than what they both had between their legs. But she writhed against him again, nipping the muscle that sloped from his neck to his shoulder and a wild primitive roar pulsed through his body.

Having sex with her all angry like this reminded him of how pissed off she'd been at him after he'd gone down on her that night at her apartment. He remembered how hard she had come and what she had tasted like. The smell of her, of them both, real and remembered, flared his nostrils and welled in his head, driving him to a point well beyond control.

In one swift movement he'd braced the flat of a forearm against the wall near her head, grasped her hip with the other hand and shoved inside her, her head rocking back as he drove in to the hilt. She cried out, her fingernails digging hard into his shoulders.

"*Yes*," she moaned, their gazes locking. "Yes."

She was hot and tight and wet, and he didn't care that he wasn't wearing a condom, he only cared that they were finally looking at each other, as close as two people could be. That he could see right into her soul and there were finally no barriers between them. He could see her emotions raw and real, the same as the ones reflected inside him. He wanted to keep her here like this, pinned to the wall in this moment of truth, this moment of utter consummation, forever.

But those fiery sparks still sizzled in Tilly's eyes, and he could tell she was mentally shrugging off the sticky tendrils of the moment.

"More," she urged, squeezing her thighs around his waist, undulating her hips, trying to buck and ride him with what little space she had available sandwiched between him and the wall.

The buzz in his balls demanded he move, too, demanded he pound into her just the way she wanted it, but his head wanted to stay in the moment for just a bit longer.

"Tanner," she moaned, nails raking down his shoulder blades now, shredding the skin.

He sucked in a breath at the pain, hot and searing. Adrenaline shot into his system, a well of anger rising like a hot geyser. "God-fucking-damn it, Matilda," he grunted through gritted teeth, staring deep into her eyes as he slid out of her and thrust back in again, rocking her head harder this time, her teeth shutting with a snap.

"Yes," she gasped triumphantly. "Yes."

And then she was incapable of forming any kind of words. He made sure of it. The only sounds coming from her mouth were insensible gasps and pants and whimpers as he pistoned his hips, rocking her higher and higher. Their gazes were locked, their breathing was tight, and their jaws were clenched as he put his shoulder into every flex of his hips, leaning heavily into the arm anchored near her head to push himself deep and hard inside her with every thrust.

She broke before he did, but just barely, finally shutting her eyes as her orgasm claimed her, the tight walls of her sex clamping down hard on his cock as she came, milking him to his own climax, sending him into the abyss with her.

Tanner barely had a chance to catch his breath before she was pushing against him. "Let me down," she said.

He roused himself, pulling his forehead off the wall, his pulse still thrumming through his ears. "I'm sorry," he murmured, easing away, his hands gentle on her hips as she slid down the wall until her feet touched the ground.

"Don't," she said, stepping around him as he tucked his dick back in his underwear. She stepped into her jeans, her back to him. "I'm not seventeen anymore. I wanted that as much as you did."

"I didn't even use a condom."

"I have an implant." She dismissed the matter, turning to face him as she zipped up her fly. "And I swear if you lie to me about having some nasty communicable disease I'm going to put that in my next feature."

Tanner's lips rose in a pained half smile. He could see the headline now. *Playboy Saint Clap King*. The rugby suits would just love that. "Nothing to worry about."

"Good," Tilly nodded, looking over his shoulder, clearly planning her escape.

"Could we please talk before you leave? About us?"

"No, Tanner," she said, her expression determined but her voice sounding sad. Or maybe just tired. "There is no us. I can't forget or forgive what you did. I thought it was bad enough that you did it, but discovering that you did it *deliberately*, that you hurt me *deliberately,* that it was pre-meditated to take my *choices* away?" Her voice was husky and tremulous now, and she sucked in a breath. "I can't be with someone who could hurt me like that and seem perfectly fine about it afterward. Could just walk away and *forget* everything we'd had. Did you ever lose any sleep over it, Tanner?"

He couldn't bear that she thought him so callous, that it was a decision he'd made lightly. He had hated himself. He took a step toward her, but she took a quick one back, holding up a hand to ward him off.

"Of course I did." He halted, shoving a hand through his hair. "I loathed myself for what I'd done."

"And yet you moved on pretty damn quickly, from what I heard. And it sure didn't seem to affect any of the rest of your life. Not the way it did me. I didn't have sex for *two years* — "

Her voice cracked and she broke off, shaking her head, her eyes big blue puddles as she stared at him. Her anguish tore at his heart. "And I've sabotaged *every* relationship I've ever had, before anyone could get too close. You've shaped me into this woman I never wanted to be. There are bits of myself I don't even *like*, while you just moved effortlessly on, swanning around with a different woman on your arm every bloody week, with clearly none of the baggage from that night."

God. He'd been such a dick—immature and rash—and he'd hurt the only woman he'd ever truly loved. "Tilly—"

She shook her head interrupting him, dashing a tear that had spilled over. "There's no *us*, Tanner. And if you ever had an ounce of compassion for me, I'm *begging* you to just *please* leave it the fuck alone."

She strode out of his room, dragging his beaten and bloody heart with her, and Tanner didn't do a damn thing to stop her. She was right. He'd hurt her, deeper than he'd known or imagined. In his eighteen-year-old brain, he'd convinced himself that she'd get over it quickly and move on, have her life, find someone else.

He'd sold her short. Sold the depth of her feelings short. And he didn't deserve her forgiveness or her love.

• • •

The fifth feature article was probably the hardest one Matilda had tackled. Had she written it *before* they'd gotten naked and done the wild thing—three times—she could have been more objective about how well-loved and respected he was by everybody. About his beautiful bromance with his teammates. About how he was cherished and doted on by the WAGS. About his generosity of spirit. But every word was coloured by what had happened that night at his apartment *after* everyone had gone home.

The sex. *And* the argument.

Objectivity was hard when so much of what she knew about Tanner Stone was viewed through the prism of her own experiences.

She must have done something right, though, because newspaper sales had spiked on the Friday of its release and it seemed everyone, everywhere, was talking about it both in the traditional media and online.

It probably had a lot to do with speculation over her and Tanner's personal relationship since his Twitter antics and that very public pash at the game last week. But even hard-as-nails Imelda Herron had stopped by her desk for some personally delivered congratulations—*a damn good story, young woman*—all but assuring Matilda she'd be moving to features permanently.

So at least something had worked out.

It was rather harder for her to shrug it all off, though, as just a damn good story. Beneath all the words, the subtext was written in tears. *Her* tears. *And blood.* If it took opening a vein and bleeding all over the page to get her where she wanted to be, she was okay with that.

But it was a double-edged sword.

Her body yearned for Tanner with the fierceness of a *woman* who was in tune with her needs. Not the girl she'd been, still learning and experimenting, still hesitant and unsure of herself and her body, slow to find her way, to be comfortable with her sexuality.

Her passion was a roaring beast inside her, sprung from its cage. But her heart was still trapped, wrapped in thorny brambles like Tanner's biceps.

Impenetrable.

She watched his next game at home alone in her pajamas, drinking beer and eating an entire large packet of salt and vinegar chips all to herself.

The WAGS wouldn't have been impressed.

She'd told herself she wasn't going to. But that was the thing with Tanner—he was addictive. And she'd just gone and overdosed on him in the worst possible way, despite warning herself from the very beginning that he was her own personal crack.

Monday morning when she reached her desk, she checked her Twitter stream to find a tweet from Tanner. He'd been quiet on social media, not entering into the speculation raging all around him and dominating his feed.

> I have perfect location for final "interview" with @MatildaK. Will text you time and place.

The tweet was depressingly void of hashtags. No #mightbelove teaser. Matilda felt curiously flat after reading it. Which was totally *crazy*. She didn't want his dumb hashtags, she didn't want to be at the centre of speculation, she didn't want there to be any implication they were an item.

Because they weren't. Nor were they going to be, either.

So she needed to snap the hell out of it.

She rifled through her bag for her phone. She usually had it on silent at work so she wouldn't have heard a text. But sure enough his name was on her screen.

Meet you at Burnside Art Collective. 5.30pm tonight.

Matilda frowned. The name was familiar because it was one of the charities she'd discovered he supported when she'd been doing her research for the article that had caused him so much consternation.

The thought of seeing him again fluttered frantically like the beating wings of a scared little bird inside her chest. She didn't want to see him again.

Surely it would be better not to put herself in the way of

temptation?

But this was work. And it was their last time. After this she need never see him again. She was going to have to suck it up and just get it done already.

She typed quickly and hit send.

See you then.

Matilda didn't know what to expect when she arrived, but it wasn't this. The large warehouse-like structure was situated in an inner city suburb caught in that halfway stage between blatant neglect and early gentrification. In a decade, it'd be one of those trendy neighbourhoods where no one could afford to live anymore, but now it was in a state of flux.

Tanner's car was already there when she pulled up, and she hurried inside. A very Zen-looking dude with tie-died pants and a grey beard so long he could plait it greeted her with clasped hands and a solemn, "*Namaste.*"

Artwork of all varieties—from paintings, sculptures and pottery, to wind chimes, gothic-looking tapestries, and large dream catchers—adorned the walls and any available surface in the large, open space. Halfway down the warehouse, a wide corridor split it in two, dividing off a series of semi-private rooms. Semi-private because there was no practical way for the walls to reach the towering roof leaving them open at the top.

Zen guy pointed down the corridor when she asked for Tanner. "Last door on the left," he murmured.

Matilda headed down the corridor, her curiosity well and truly piqued. She hadn't looked into the specifics of Tanner's involvement with this particular not-for-profit when she'd been investigating his charity works. She'd mainly focused on the big name ones. The fact that he was supporting the arts, the opposite end of the spectrum to rugby, was very interesting indeed.

When she reached the room, she was surprised to read the sign on the door announcing it to be the Matilda's Muse literacy programme for girls. The sign also said it had been established five years ago.

Matilda blinked, her heart squeezing in her chest.

She opened the door, and about two-dozen faces turned to check out the intruder. The girls, who all looked to be about eleven or twelve, sat around desks that accommodated four or five. Each participant had paper and pens in front of them.

Tanner glanced at her from his position lounging against the back wall. He smiled at her, then at the twenty-something young woman in front, who'd paused mid-sentence, waving at her to continue.

"Hey," he whispered as he drew closer and the speaker picked up her thread. He was in jeans again, with a T-shirt that showed off his muscular physique to perfection. Something stirred deep in her belly. Some kind of primal recognition. Some weird wild pheromone thing.

As if he'd imprinted himself on her when he'd been deep inside her the other night.

"Come stand at the back."

Confused, Matilda followed him. They lounged against the wall again, and it took her a moment to realise the identity of the woman who was talking.

"That's Andrea Willoughby," Matilda whispered.

Andrea was an up and coming YA writer whose book about a teenage girl who saves the human race had just been optioned for a movie. Her audience was listening with rapt attention.

"Yes," he agreed, dropping the whisper but keeping his voice low. "Thought she might be a hit with the class."

She absorbed the information and the scene for a while. "This is your baby?" she asked eventually, also dropping to a whisper, glancing at his profile for confirmation.

"Yes."

He didn't look at her or bother to elaborate. Yet there was pride in his voice. He'd established this? "Why?"

He shrugged, rolling his head to the side, their gazes meeting. "Because I remember how much you were into reading and writing, and how much you would have killed to have access to writing classes and mentoring opportunities. I wanted to try and foster the kind of talent you always had. To inspire and nurture it."

A rush of emotion bubbled in her chest. "Matilda's Muse," she uttered.

He rolled his head back to the midline, returning his attention to the guest speaker now. "How could I call it anything else?"

The quiet sincerity of his voice hit her hard, and a block of sudden emotion in her chest balled into a big fat lump, threatening to crush her ribs and cut off the breath in her throat.

He'd established a literacy programme for talented young women. *In her honour?* That was about the nicest, sweetest, most awesome thing any guy had ever done.

He rolled his head to the side again, leaning in, their arms brushing, his mouth close to her ear, his voice low. "I never *forgot* you, Tilly. I never just walked away. You were always on my mind." He dropped his voice to a whisper. "I never stopped loving you."

A tear Matilda didn't even know had been building slid down her face. *He loved her.* Those words should be joyful, but all she felt was pain. Him loving her didn't matter. He took her choice away, and she couldn't forgive him for that. Maybe she'd have followed him, maybe she wouldn't have.

But it had been *her* decision to make—not his.

There may have been a lot of good in the way things had panned out *and* in Tanner's reasoning, but right now it just felt like she'd been punished. For loving him too much. For wanting too much.

And it hurt.

"But *I* stopped loving you," she whispered.

And she had. It had been the hardest thing she'd done, but she'd excised him from her life. Or so she'd thought. Already she could feel the rekindling of old emotions and she couldn't go there again. She had to deal them a swift blow—for both their sakes.

If his slumped shoulders and the disbelief in his eyes were anything to go by, her mission was accomplished.

Good. It was imperative she destroyed any hopes he might have that she felt something for him, that they might get back together.

Destroy them as he had destroyed her hopes all those years ago.

What had he said? *Smash a gulf so wide…*

She locked her gaze with his. "Good-bye, Tanner."

She pushed off the wall and headed for the door, her hands shaking as she escaped into the corridor, tears streaming down her face as she hurried from the building, dashed to her car, and locked herself inside. She gripped the steering wheel hard, staring through the windscreen at the front door, willing it to open, willing Tanner to appear. Her foolish, *contrary* heart hoping desperately that he'd seen through her bravado and would refuse to take no for an answer.

If he came for her now, with the heavy dread of finality sitting like an elephant on her chest, she wouldn't have the power to resist.

She waited for fifteen minutes, tears falling freely, but he didn't appear. She guessed there were only so many times she could push him away before he stopped pushing back.

She started the car and slowly drove away, her head stoic, her heart a mess.

Chapter Fifteen

"So then, out with it," Hannah Kent said as Matilda handed her a coffee and sat on the chair next to hers on the back porch.

There were damn reminders of Tanner everywhere.

Matilda frowned. "What?"

Hannah shot her an incredulous look. "I'm old, not stupid, girlie. You know how much I love seeing you, but it's Wednesday. You *never* come on Wednesday. And you're moping around here like you just lost your best friend."

Matilda's stomach lurched. *It felt like she had.* "I'm just preoccupied," she evaded. "With work."

There was an elegant snort to her left. "With Tanner, you mean?"

Well, yes. Tanner *was* work. "Kind of," she evaded. "I've started the last feature article half a dozen times. I just can't seem to get it right."

"And is there a particular reason why you're not at his place discussing this? Drinking coffee with him? In his bed maybe? You know, like naked? Making me great-grandbabies?"

"Gran." Matilda didn't think that the warning note in her

voice would be paid much heed but she injected it anyway.

"He's always been the one for you, Matilda. So, it didn't work out when you're younger." She shrugged. "Doesn't mean it won't now. I could tell with my own two eyes he's still carrying a torch for you. Blind Freddy can see that."

A spike of annoyance flushed through Matilda veins. Her grandmother had always had a soft spot for Tanner. "And do you know why it didn't work out?" she demanded.

Her grandmother didn't seem too perturbed by Matilda's crankiness. "Why don't you tell me?"

So she did. She told her grandmother everything. About that night and the kiss and how she'd just learned it was a deliberate action by Tanner to break them up. About how hurt she'd been then and how betrayed she felt now.

Hannah waited for her to finally come to a halt and calmly asked, "So?"

Matilda blinked. "What do you mean, *so*?"

"If he hadn't broken up with you, would you have knocked back your scholarship?"

Matilda opened her mouth to tell her grandmother that it was beside the point, but shut it again as Hannah held up her hand and said, "No. Just *think* about it for a moment. Forget the emotions of that time, what are the facts?" Despite her affront, the question sunk its claws into Matilda's brain. "And be *honest*," her grandmother added, capturing Matilda's gaze.

Peering back to that time eight years ago had always been a painful experience. Now it was uncomfortable as well, being forced to take out the feelings and step back and look at it with objectivity.

There was only one person on the entire planet she'd do it for.

What *were* the facts? Matilda wished she could shy from them but the truth was, she had been deadly serious about her intention to knock back that scholarship. Tanner had urged—

begged—her not to, but she'd been adamant. She'd loved him so much, she hadn't been able to bear the thought of being away from him for even a day, let alone three years.

Matilda dropped her gaze to her coffee. "Yes."

"Right, well," Hannah said, plonking her mug down on the table between them. "I, for one, am glad he did." Her tone was brisk and no-nonsense. "If I'd have known you were even *considering* giving up on your dream, I'd have kicked your backside all the way to Stanford. It seems like I have a lot to thank Tanner Stone for."

If Matilda thought she was going to get sympathy from her grandmother, she thought wrong. Hannah Kent had never been one of those over-indulgent grandmothers. Sure, she had Matilda's back, but she wasn't so one-eyed that she couldn't see both sides of a story.

"Can you honestly sit here and tell me," her grandmother continued, clearly on a roll, "that if you had your time over again that you'd not want to do Stanford? That you'd take back all those experiences you had, and all those people you've met, and all the contacts you made, and all the fun you had over there, and all those dreams you dreamed…to follow a *boy* around?"

Hannah made her sound incredibly flaky and naive, but it hadn't just been some guy she'd had a crush on. It hadn't just been *any* boy. It had been Tanner. And she'd been in love with him.

"He did you a huge favour there, girlie."

It was Matilda's turn to snort. "By smashing my heart into a million pieces?" she demanded. "By publically humiliating me?"

"Oh, for goodness sake," Hannah said snippily, rising to her feet to frown down at her granddaughter. "He was *eighteen.* A teenager. A teenage *boy.* Everybody knows ninety percent of their thinking is carried out by their peckers. So, he made a hash of it." She shrugged. "He hurt you and I'm sorry. But I seem to remember you making a hash out of quite a few things when you were a teenager. You're twenty-six years old, Matilda. Should you *still* have to pay for them?"

Matilda remembered a few of those incidents, and her cheeks warmed. Her grandmother had the uncanny knack of getting right to the heart of the matter. She'd always hated that about the old biddy. Matilda had never thought of herself as petty or judgemental, but that was exactly the way Hannah was making her feel.

"I suppose not."

"And correct me if I'm wrong," Hannah went on, pressing her advantage, "but Tanner's spent an awful lot of his time these last weeks trying to show you he's not that kid anymore, yes? Maybe you could cut him a little slack?"

Matilda should have known not to come to her grandmother's for pity. She should have known she'd only get honesty. Maybe that was why she *was* here. For honesty.

"You think I've been too harsh on him."

"I think the only question that really matters is why? Why are you so het up about it all still? Surely after *eight years* you've moved on from all that, and if so, then why does it matter so much? Unless you still love him? Do you?"

Matilda hadn't been feeling particularly emotional. She'd mostly been annoyed by her grandmother's deep streak of fairness that had weighted the scales in Tanner's favour. But the question hit her hard, cracking the denial she'd been holding in check since Tanner had walked back into her life.

"Yes."

Suddenly, her face was crumpling, and her grandmother was beside her, sliding an arm around her shoulder, drawing Matilda's head to her waist, patting her arm, and making soothing noises.

"Well, go and get him, girlie. Life's too short to hold on to old grudges. Time to let go of the past."

Matilda shut her eyes as the tears streamed down her face. It sounded so easy. But had she blown it for good?

• • •

When Matilda finally made it home, she walked through her door with absolute purpose. She loved Tanner, and she wanted him back. Her talk with Gran, and some thinking time on her drive home, had crystallised it all.

Gran, with her usual cut-through-the-bullshit style of diplomacy, had been right. They'd been teenagers, and yes, Tanner had made a hash of it. But his intentions had been good, and they were adults now. If she wanted to have a future with him—and God help her, she *did*—she had to get over the past. She had to let all that shit go to move on.

She had to forgive him for the hurt and understand that it hadn't been intentional, that he'd done what he'd done for all the right reasons.

He'd forced her to follow her dreams because she wouldn't have. And *that* was the truth of it.

Gran was right—she did have him to thank for that. Now, she had to get him back.

And she knew how to go about it.

If there was one thing Matilda was good at, it was words. On paper, anyway. Her oral communication with him had clearly, thus far, sucked. So that was how she would reach him. She had one more piece to write, and she had to make it count.

Whether he'd fall for it, of course, after her rejection of him at the art collective on Monday—the last in a string of rejections—was a completely different matter.

But she was going to give it her best damn shot.

She went straight to her computer. The words, which had

been stubbornly absent before, flew from her fingers. The piece was an utterly personal perspective of the man. Tanner through her eyes. It talked about growth and change and the passage of time. It talked about the boy she'd known versus the legend of today. It talked about sacrifice and courage and forgiveness.

About a man bigger than the myth.

She wrote for two hours without looking up, tinkering and editing, deleting and adding, until she had it perfect. But it needed one more thing.

Something to take it from a slightly personal feature article to a...love letter.

A public declaration.

A couple of weeks ago, Tanner Stone famously kicked three field goals for my favour. But past hurts and insecurities are hard beasts to master, and I sent him on his way. I was wrong. The truth is, I'm older, and I'm wiser, and I know the difference between reckless and real. So now here I am, standing in front of all of you and a set of metaphorical goal posts, with a ball and ten seconds before the final hooter, asking him *for* his *favour. Asking for his forgiveness. Giving him mine in return.*

You said once you wanted to marry me. I still do. #definitelylove

Matilda's cheeks were wet as she typed THE END, desperately hoping it *wasn't* their end, but a beginning.

Whether Imelda Herron and the paper would indulge her with this final piece, particularly with that ending, she had no idea. But she had to try.

Asking him to marry her? Cheesy, yes. Desperate, *hell yes*. But perfect. She wanted forever from him, and she wanted him to know it in no uncertain terms.

Nothing ventured. Nothing gained.

• • •

As it turned out, Imelda and the powers that be, already high on the outstanding sales numbers generated by the intense media speculation over Tanner and Matilda, were more than thrilled to print Matilda's piece with absolutely no changes.

It was the first time she'd ever seen Imelda in raptures. "And in a leap year, too," she'd enthused.

But when Friday rolled around, Matilda was like a cat on a hot tin roof. The article was an instant hit—her proposal, it seemed, going viral—but she felt ill sitting at her desk, screening hundreds of "can we please get a comment" phone calls for the one that really mattered.

Tanner's call.

Which never came.

Twitter—his social media platform of choice—was going off. His followers must have been wearing their thumbs to the bone in their tweeting frenzy.

One of the many tweets from rugbybunny1 read:

#holysmoke @MatildaK you go girlfriend #TannMat #justsayyes

And from slickstonesmistress:

#holysmoke Looks like someone hasn't been wearing her #kryptonitepanties!! Its ok @MatildaK, am prepared to share my man with you.

Hell, #TannMat and #justsayyes trended for hours. But Tanner was eerily silent.

By the end of the day, after stalking Twitter, Facebook, Tumblr, and Instagram, and checking her phone about a hundred times, Matilda had to admit she really *had* blown it. Had he read the article, or was he still too mad at her to even do that? But how could someone so active on social media miss the viral response to it?

Which meant he'd seen it and was ignoring it, or he was too embarrassed or too furious to speak.

By the time she got home on Friday night, she had to face facts. He wasn't going to reply. She'd screwed up that day at the art collective. Telling him she'd stopped loving him, *not* telling him that she'd started again, actively *denying* her love to both of them—she'd pushed him away for good.

She went straight to the fridge, cracked open the lid on the bottle of white wine that had been sitting there since Christmas because it had been a cheap and nasty freebie from a stingy secret Santa, and swigged it straight from the bottle. She winced and screwed up her face at the vinegar edge to it but took another swig as she reached for a silver-foiled family block of fruit-and-nut chocolate and gnawed off the corner.

The sweetness—especially after gnawing off the other corner—overrode the sourness of the wine. Not that she cared. It was one of those nights. She was going to take her contacts out, put on her baggy pants, eat chocolate, and watch *The Sound of Music*—an era where a nun could fall in love with a naval captain without the aid of freaking *Twitter*—all while getting resoundingly drunk.

Three hours later, with still no word from Tanner, she staggered to bed having accomplished everything she'd set out to do. Lying in the dark, with no singing nun for distraction, the tears came and she didn't bother to stop them. In the morning, she'd get her shit sorted and figure out another way to reach Tanner. Something bigger and grander.

A skywriter maybe.

Or a blimp.

But right now, she wanted to continue her pity party. So she cried. And she cried some more. In fact, she cried herself to sleep.

Chapter Sixteen

Tanner was running late for the Smoke's Saturday morning training session as the Uber he was in pulled away from the air field and headed for Henley stadium. They didn't usually train on Saturdays because, more often than not it was game day, but this week they had a Sunday game and, given it was against their toughest opponents to date, Griff had insisted on the session.

Knowing Griff, he probably wouldn't stop until the will to live had been wrung out of every single one of them.

Tanner drummed his fingers on his jeans, feeling naked without his phone. He'd accidentally left it behind in his locker on Thursday and hadn't realised it until he was almost at the airport for his trip west. But, given there was no mobile reception way out where he'd been heading, and the retreat for young male offenders was completely unplugged anyway — no phones, no computers, no television — it had been pointless going back for it.

Still, he felt like he'd been away from civilisation for a month, despite it only being a day and a half. He was desperate to check his messages and his Twitter stream and extra desperate to read Tilly's last feature article, even though the crushing sense that there truly was no hope left for them had been on his mind since Monday.

Still…he couldn't help himself where she was concerned.

Being seven hundred kilometres away, in the middle of nowhere, mentoring a bunch of guys who'd done it really tough had been a good distraction. They had given Tanner something to focus on other than obsessing about Tilly's last words.

Yeah, but I stopped loving you.

Except now he was back again, in civilisation, and the words were back, playing over and over in his head.

If it was true—and she'd said it with such convincing sincerity—then he only had himself to blame. But he wasn't giving up, either. He loved her, and he couldn't just switch those feelings off.

He needed to give her some time, however. Give them *both* some time. Then start as friends. And take it slow.

She'd fallen for him once. Surely she could again.

All the guys were in the locker room when he burst through the door almost an hour later. Traffic had been a nightmare, and he had five minutes to spare before Griff would be in the room and have his ass if he wasn't kitted up and ready to go.

"Well, look who the cat dragged in," Dex said with a grin. "So glad you could make it."

"The man of the moment," Linc announced.

"Nah," Bodie added, "The man bigger than the myth."

Tanner frowned, ignoring them. He didn't have time to try and decipher their bullshit right now. He had to get dressed and get his head in the game. He hurried to his locker, yanking his shirt over his head as he went, pulling up short at the newspaper article stuck to the front with electrical tape. It was Matilda's last feature. The headline read TANNER STONE, A MAN BIGGER THAN THE MYTH. And, lower down, there was a ring of bright red Nikko around the very last sentence.

You said once you wanted to marry me, Tanner. I still do. #definitelylove

What the fuck? Tanner's pulse spiked, and his hands trembled as he tore it off the locker to read it. He devoured the article, not looking up until "The End." It was then he realised there was absolute silence in the room, and he glanced over his shoulder.

All the guys were grinning like loons, and Dex and Donovan took two paces forward and tossed handfuls of confetti at Tanner's stunned face. Linc hummed the wedding march. "Da dum da da. Da dum da da. Da dum da da da da da da da."

"I bag best men," Bodie said.

"In your fucking dreams," Dex said good-naturedly.

Tanner, his head spinning, glanced back at the article. She'd really just proposed to him in a *national newspaper*?

"What are you waiting for?" Dex demanded. "Don't keep the lady waiting. We like her better than you."

"Yeah," Linc agreed. "She's hella prettier to look at than you, too."

Tanner grinned, his heart suddenly light as a freaking balloon. The heavy weight he'd carried all week suddenly lifted. He stuffed the newspaper article in his pocket and shoved his shirt back on over his head, displacing a bunch of confetti.

He reached into his locker, grabbed his phone, and was heading for the door when Griff sauntered in. He took one look at Tanner, dressed in civvies and folded his arms across his chest. His gaze skimmed Tanner's confetti-strewn hair before coming to a halt on his face.

"And where the fuck do you think you're going?"

"Sorry, Griff. There's a personal matter I have to attend to."

Griff was unmoved. "You already missed yesterday's training."

Tanner reefed the crumpled up article out his pocket. "Gotta go accept a proposal of marriage, boss."

"It can't wait?" he demanded.

"I've already waited eight years."

Griff rolled his eyes. "This is the kind of shit I expect from Linc."

"Hey," Linc protested not looking remotely insulted.

Griff pinned Tanner with a steely gaze. "You going to bring your A game tomorrow?"

He nodded. "Yes, sir." Tilly and rugby were all he needed.

Griff stood aside. "Go."

A cacophony of male hooting followed him out of the locker room.

. . .

Matilda woke with a start at ten in the morning. Her head throbbed, her eyes were gritty in the way only hours of crying produced, and it tasted like a small, furry animal had died in her mouth overnight. She groaned as she rolled on her back.

Drinking the entire bottle of wine last night hadn't been very smart.

She searched blindly in her bedside table drawer for a box of breath mints she knew was in there somewhere, finally locating them and throwing three in her mouth. Next she groped for her phone and found her glasses, shoving them on her face as she struggled to her elbows, half-sitting.

Maybe there'd been some news from Tanner overnight?

She peered blearily at the phone screen, tapping in her

passcode. A hot well of disappointment fountained in her chest to find no missed phone calls. No texts.

The urge to cry returned, but she beat it back. Crying was for last night.

No more bloody crying.

She quickly navigated to Twitter. As there were yesterday, several hundred notifications awaited her. But were any from Tanner? Rather than searching through them all she cut to the chase and went straight to his profile.

She almost dropped the phone when she saw his one and only tweet in days sent out about an hour ago.

Yes @MatildaK #Istilldotoo #definitelylove

There were hundreds of retweets and responses beneath, none of which she cared about as the news took long seconds to set in. *Yes?* Her heart raced, her breath caught around a giant lump in her throat threatening to choke her.

He said yes?

A low buzz of excitement that seemed to originate from the phone spread from the tips of her fingers, down her arms to her chest and belly, then down her legs, all the way to her toes.

He said yes. Definitely love!

She grinned at the phone like a madwoman, her heart practically floating in her chest, then promptly burst into tears.

So much for that!

A loud banging on her front door startled her, causing her to almost choke on her breath mints. "Tilly! It's me. It's Tanner! Open up!"

Tanner?

Matilda's pulse leaped as she practically levitated from the bed. If she'd had her wits about her, she might have cared that she was in a T-shirt that said "Journalists do it on the front page," instead of her slinky, clingy red lace negligee. Or that her eyes were probably bloodshot to hell, and her hair probably looked more punk than pixie. Or that she probably still stunk of booze.

All she cared about was getting her hands on her man.

Her man.

She could get used to that.

She was at the door in ten seconds flat, her hand fumbling with the dead lock. Then it was open and he was standing there in a pair of knee-length chinos and a T-shirt soaked in sweat. More sweat poured down his forehead and neck, his golden-blond hair dark at the roots where perspiration had saturated it in clumps.

"Yes," he said grinning at her. "Yes."

Matilda didn't care how sweaty he was. She threw herself at him, crawling up him to kiss him on the mouth, whispering, "Yes, yes, yes," against his lips.

Somehow they ended up inside her apartment on the other side of her door, pressed against it, kissing like they'd never kissed before, like the world was about to end and this was the way they'd chosen to spend their last moment.

"I love you," she said eventually, sinking her hands into his sweaty hair, pressing her forehead to his as she sucked in lungsful of much needed air.

"I love you, too," he said simply.

"God," she said, on a half laugh. "You sure as hell played it cool. I thought I'd blown it."

"No." He shook his head. "I'm sorry. I've been in the far west of the state, unplugged since Thursday afternoon. I only saw the article about an hour ago."

"So you…" She brushed his sweaty fringe off his forehead. "You ran all the way here?"

"Practically. I got caught in a traffic gridlock due to some accident. Nobody could go anywhere so I mounted the kerb, parked the car, and ran the last eight kilometres."

Matilda laughed incredulous. "That's crazy."

He shook his head. "No. It's the sanest thing I've ever done." He kissed her again, and Matilda's heart sang as she held him tight. "Do you have a shower in this place?"

She grinned at him as she wriggled down. "Follow me."

A trail of their clothes lay strewn on the floor by the time they both hit the shower, completely naked. Tanner turned on the cold only, and Matilda gasped but he soon wrapped her up in his arms and kissed her senseless against the tile, urging her to wrap her legs around his waist.

But she refused to go, turning him so his back was to the tile instead and kissing down his chest. And down lower. And lower.

"Tilly," he said, pulling gently on her shoulders. "I want to be in you."

"Later," she said, rising on her tiptoes to place a playful kiss on his mouth before sinking to her knees in front of him.

Cold water sprayed down all around her, beading her nipples to tight points, and her head was level with the thick, long jut of his erection. She looked up at him, past the flat of his belly, the spread of his ribs, the wide expanse of his chest, the whiskery length of his neck, the brooding line of his mouth.

All the way up to the lust-fuelled blue of his eyes. "I want to taste you."

The rings of cartilage in his throat bobbed as he swallowed. "You can have whatever you want. I'm all yours."

Matilda smiled at him, pressing her knees into the grout of the tile in case she actually become so light with happiness she floated. "Good answer."

Then she grasped the base of his cock in one hand, cupped his balls with the other and sunk her lips down his shaft, taking him right to the back of her throat.

She just heard the *thunk* of his head against the tile over the sound of the water and his long, low, "*Fuuuck.*"

A surge of pure feminine power streaked through her system, and Matilda withdrew, sucking hard all the way before eating him up again, going as far as she could, alternately squeezing and rolling his balls.

She glanced up to find him, head back, eyes closed, his palms flattened hard against the tiles behind him, his knuckles white as if he was trying to stop himself from moving or touching her. But Matilda wanted him to move. To thrust. She wanted him to touch her. She wanted to feel his hands on her head, in her hair, urging her on.

She wanted him to *watch* her blowing him, watch her making him come with her mouth, watch her swallow everything he had to give.

She withdrew all the way, letting the plump head sit gently against her lips. He roused shortly, his eyes fluttering open before he looked down.

"I want you to watch me," she said, her voice husky. "Hold my head. Guide me."

His low groan went straight to her belly, and she swore she could see the tightening of his abs. His gaze fixed on hers as his hands slid into her hair, and she felt the subtle pressure of them as they urged her back onto his cock.

Matilda shut her eyes in deep satisfaction, opening to take him all, moaning as he thrust slightly to push deeper, protesting as he pulled out then sucking greedily as he thrust in again.

Now they were a team. It wasn't just her on her knees servicing him. *He* was a part of it. Fucking her mouth. And she freaking loved it. He was hot and slippery against her tongue, tasting like salt and musk, the chill of the water lubricating and cooling all at once.

When his legs started to tremble, she knew he was nearly

there. His balls drew tighter, and he started to thrust faster. Matilda matched him, sucking harder and faster, clawing at the back of his thighs to stop herself from dissolving into a puddle of lust and washing down the drain.

"*Oh…yes…baby*," he muttered, his hands clamping in her hair, his hips suddenly jerking to a stop. A deep bellow echoed around the shower as his hot seed spilled into her mouth. She swallowed until he was spent, clinging to his legs as he eased from her mouth, pressing her forehead to his thigh as blood pounded through her head.

"Come here," he said after a beat, reaching down for her, hauling her up his body as the cool water flowed down her back before he turned her around. Her legs automatically wrapped around his hips as he leaned heavily against her like he was having trouble holding himself up.

"That was amazing," he muttered, before his mouth descended hot and a little crazy on hers. "God," he groaned. "Tasting me on you is such a frickin' turn-on."

Matilda laughed, her heart about as full as it could possibly be. "I know how you feel."

He nuzzled her neck for a moment, obviously needing some recovery time. "Why'd you change your mind?" he asked, his voice muffled.

Matilda stared into the water spurting out of the showerhead. "Because we were kids but now we're adults, and it was well past time for me to get over it. Because your intentions were good, even if your execution sucked. And because as much as I didn't still want to love you…I still did."

He lifted his head from her neck. "I *am* sorry," he murmured, his blue eyes earnest, despite the sexy cling of water droplets.

"I know." She pressed a soft kiss to his mouth. "So am I." And she kissed him again. "Are you sure about the getting married thing? I kind of put you on the spot a bit there. We don't have to. We can take it slow, see how it goes."

"No way." Tanner shook his head emphatically, the water droplets flying from the ends of his hair and his eyelashes. "I've waited eight years for this, and I'm not wasting another minute. This isn't maybe love or probably love or even definitely love anymore. This is *forever* love, and I want that to start right here, right now. Today."

Matilda grinned at him. "Forever love?" Exactly what she wanted from him. "Can we hashtag that?"

"Sure." He grinned back. "Later. Right now there's another hashtag on my mind." He unlocked her ankles from around his hips, eased her legs to the ground then dropped to his knees in front of her as she had done to him.

Matilda's heart skipped a beat.

"Hold on, baby," he said, gripping her right leg, bending it at the knee and urging it up and over his shoulder, splaying her wide open before him. "Captain Cunnilingus is in da house."

Matilda gasped and shut her eyes as he put his mouth to her. She pushed a hand into his wet hair, her body coming alive, her heart glowing big and bright and full in her chest.

Forever love was going to be freaking awesome.

Glossary

I've probably used some words in here that some readers may not know—both rugby ones and strange Aussie-isms alike. So I thought a handy dandy glossary might help. It is, of course, written entirely from my perspective so is heavily biased, female-centric, and quite possibly dodgy. It probably wouldn't stand up to any kind of official scrutiny...

Footy – We love this term in Australia. The confusing thing for most non-Aussies is they never know which game it refers to because we have three separate but distinct codes of football in Australia:

    1. Rugby League (Jarryd Hayne played this code before he went and played Gridiron).

    2. Rugby union – The code the Sydney Smoke play and the one this series is based upon (Jarryd Hayne now trying his hand at this code as well...).

    3. Aussie rules football – Different altogether. Tall, fit guys in *really* tight shorts.

    There is also soccer but we don't really think of that as

football in the traditional sense here in Australia.

The confusing thing is we refer to all of them as *the footy* e.g. "Wanna go to the footy, Davo?" And somehow we all seem to know which code is being referred to at any given time. Even more confusing, the ball that is used in each code is often also called the footy e.g. "Chuck me *the footy*, Gazza."

Pitch – Apparently the rugby field is called a pitch but colloquially here we just call it the footy (see, I told you we liked that term) field. A pitch is more a cricket term. No, don't worry, I won't ever try to explain a game that lasts five days to you…

Ruck – No, not a typo. That's ruck with an R, ladies! Happens after a tackle as each team tries to gain possession of the ball.

Line-out – That weird thing they use to restart play where each team lines up side by side, vertical to the sideline, and one of the guys throws the ball to his team and a few of the guys from that team bodily lift one dude up to snatch the ball out of the air. It's like rugby ballet. Minus the tutus. And usually with more blood.

Scrum – Another way to gain possession of the ball. I'm going to paraphrase several definitions I've read: A scrum is when two groups of opposing players pack loosely together, arms interlocked, heads down, jockeying for the ball that is fed into the scrum along the ground. It's like a tug of war with no rope and more body contact or, as I like to call it, a great big man hug with a lot of dudes lying on top of each other at the end of it all. Very homoerotic. Win/win.

Try – A goal. Except in rugby union we don't say someone scored a goal, we say someone scored a try after they've dived for the line and a bunch of other guys have jumped on top to try and stop it from happening. Very homoerotic. Win/win. A try is worth five points.

Haka – A ceremonial dance performed by all Polynesian cultures but made famous by the New Zealand All Blacks rugby team who perform it before every match in an awesome, spine chilling display of power, passion, and identity. I'm sure it's only coincidental that it's also crap-your-pants scary. There are few things more fearsome than an advancing All Black haka!

WAG – Wives and girlfriends. These are partners of the dudes that play rugby. Although we also use the term here in Oz to refer to partners of our cricket players. I think in the UK WAGS is also a term used for football (soccer) partners.

Pash – Not a footy term but one I used a couple of times which confused the heck out of my editor. A pash is a kiss e.g. "Did you pash him, Shazza." It's the Aussie equivalent to the British term snog.

Acknowledgments

My thanks, as always must go to all the team at Entangled, particularly those who work on the Brazen imprint. You are all superstars.

Extra special thanks to two gorgeous men who are my rugby gurus and the guys I go to for much needed info as I write this series. To David Grice and Jon O'Brien who, between them, have answered my crazy queries via text day and night. Questions about rucks (*not* a typo), hooters (no, not *those* kind), blood rules, goals, tries, salaries, those weird line out thingies…the list goes on. These two men—husbands of dear friends—are on speed dial and will be for as long as this series continues. I'm not sure they fully knew what they got themselves into when they agreed to be my rugby guides… but I am forever grateful to both of them.

About the Author

Multi-award-winning and USA Today bestselling author Amy Andrews is an Aussie who has written fifty romances, from novellas to category to single-title in both the traditional and digital markets for a variety of publishers. Her first love is steamy contemporary romance that makes her readers tingle, laugh, and sigh. At the age of sixteen, she met a guy she instantly knew she was going to marry, so she just smiles when people tell her insta-love books are unrealistic because she did marry that man and, twenty-odd years later, they're still living out their happily ever after.

She loves good books, fab food, great wine, and frequent travel—preferably all four together. She lives on acreage on the outskirts of Brisbane with a gorgeous mountain view but secretly wishes it were the hillsides of Tuscany.

If you love sexy romance, one-click these steamy Brazen releases...

ONE WEEK TO SCORE
a *Tall, Dark, and Texan* novel by Kate Meader

Olivia Kane's wedding day has just imploded spectacularly. What her pity party does not need is six feet and change of home-grown Texas cockiness in the form of her brother's best friend. But Flynn Cross won't stand by while Liv finds sensual solace in the arms of a stranger. Not when his own hard-for-her body is more than up for the task...

ENGAGING THE BACHELOR
a *Pulse* novel by Cathryn Fox

Hot, Southampton doctor, Carson Reynolds isn't the kind of man Gemma Carr should be playing with. But his offer of a fake engagement comes with sexy, late night house calls, and despite her bad girl reputation, it's been far too long since she's taken two and called anyone in the morning. But is she asking for a prescription for trouble?

HIS FANTASY BRIDE
a *Things To Do Before You Die* novel by Nina Croft

Vito D' Ascensio is the one man Gabby Harper can never have, but as desire explodes between them, she has a tough time remembering why they shouldn't be together. Oh, right, her family hates him, and he's done terrible things. Or has he? But it doesn't matter. When he finds out the truth about who she really is…he'll never want to see her again.

WRONG BED REUNION
a *Most Likely To* novel by Candy Sloane

Georgia Cahill is at her high school reunion to seduce the quarterback boyfriend she left behind ten years ago. Unfortunately, one too many margaritas accidentally land her in bed with Gideon Neill, the class geek, instead. By the time she realizes her mistake, she's the one being seduced.